i

Shani Greene Dowdell

Presents

Keepin' It Tight

A

Shanibooks Publication

www.shanibooks.com

Keepin' It Tight is a work of fiction. All characters, plots and situations are a figment of the author's imagination. Any references or similarities to actual events, real people, living or dead, or to real locales are intended to give the novel a sense of reality. Any similarity in other names, characters, places, and incidents are entirely coincidental.

Publisher: Shanibooks
Lulu Content Number: 539687
ISBN: 978-0-6151-5074-1

Cover Design: Chanel Smith (www.web-presence-designs.com)
Photography compliments of istockphoto.com (Sharon Dominick, Justin Horrocks, Pixlmaker)

Printed in the United States of America

Dedication

This book is dedicated to my loved ones who crossed over before this project could be completed. I'll see you at the crossroads.

Charles Wilmington Greene,
Kenneth Dowdell,
and
Shareef Abdullah, Jr.,
You will hold
A special place
In my heart.
Always

Acknowledgements

My journey to becoming a published author has not been easy, but had it not been for the support that I have received along the way I would not be where I am today.

Thanks to God for allowing my dream to come true, and for speaking to my spirit when I felt like giving up.

Thanks to my editors, Carla Dean and Christopher Greene, for doing such a great job helping me get Keepin' It Tight polished up.

This has been a loooooooong bumpy ride for my family, but at the finish line the reward is sweet. Thanks to my husband, Anthony (Bootsy) Dowdell, who has been patient most days and stood over my shoulder while I attempted to complete a chapter or two on others. Either way, thanks for staying by my side through this journey. You know I love you, Bootsy.

Kimbria, Athena, and Anthony, thanks for helping momma out by keeping your chores done, helping select my book cover, and being so understanding as I spent hours at my computer working on Keepin' It Tight. I love and appreciate each one of you. You all have a light to shine on this world, so always be true to yourselves and follow your dreams

I want to shout out to all of my aunts and uncles: Gwendolyn Purter, Cheryl Greene, Charles Greene, Stephanie Terry, Rex Greene, Christopher Greene, Louise Abdullah, Brenda Woods, Denise McNeil, Carla McNeil, Michael McNeil, and Melvin Freeman. Each of you had a unique hand in helping raise me. THANK YOU! (You too, Shareef)

To my great grandmother (Madea), thank you for your pearls of wisdom along the way. A lot of the woman who I am today, I owe to you.

To my grandmothers Betty Greene and Lillie Pearl Robinson. Two women that I can't see myself living without, I love you.

Valerie Ball, my mother, thanks for always pushing me to heights I never knew I could reach. I love you momma (and yeah, I'm going back to nursing school one day soon :). To Michael Ball, my stepfather, your encouragement really means a lot to me. It's people like you that feed the soul of a dreamer like myself.

To my father, Caron Knox, thanks for always holding a special place in your heart for me. You took a fatherless child like myself and embraced me like your own. Thanks for your continued support and presence in my life. I love you and Mrs. Lou.

To Lewis and Jacquelyn Dowdell, my father and mother in law, who treat me just like I'm the daughter they never had, I love you guys!

Thanks Felicia Chislom for all of your ideas and encouragement of this book's storyline. You have been there since day one, when writing a book was just another one of our pipe dreams. Come on, I'm waiting to be acknowledged in your book next.

Tiffany, Jerrick, Kevin (a.k.a Kelli-Kev), Doug, Jennifer, Alex (can't wait to see you walk across that stage December 2007 – congrats on getting that degree lil bro), Jeromy (a.k.a. Big Heert) my sisters and brothers, I love you guys. You have been so supportive, some calling me the next Terry McMillan and hyping me up. Stop blowing my head up – on the other hand do go on! I hope Keepin' It Tight will live up to your expectations (Kelli-Kev, I know you say as soon as it's a movie you're going to watch it, lol, but big bro, you better read my book!)

Thanks to my friends who showed support along the way: Joi Marsh, Tisha Renee Baldwin-McConnell, Sherika Mennifield, Nikki Brown and Deborah May.

Fellow authors: Naiomi Pitre, Darrien Lee, Leila Jefferson, Kisha Green, CJ Domino, Claudia Brown Mosley, DL Sparks, Therone Shellman, Jade Alex, Kerry E. Wagner, just to name a few of the authors I admire. Thank you for your advice, guidance, inspiration or just being a listening ear over the past year. Your wealth of information and nurturing have been priceless to a wet-behind-the-ear author like myself.

And last but not least, to you, my readers, thank you wholeheartedly for supporting my work. The love and support that I'm getting on my debut is humbling to say the least.

If I forgot someone, you know I didn't mean to, charge it to my mind not my heart.

If you are online feel free to visit me:
www.shanibooks.com.
www.myspace.com/shanibouttoblowup.
www.shanibooks.blogspot.com.
http://groups.yahoo.com/group/shanibooks/join.
Feel free to email me at sdowdell30@yahoo.com with comments. Go to amazon.com, lulu.com, or bn.com and leave a review. Then, good people, *go buy some books!*

Prologue

Lela James had all but given up on true love. Her theory was that "true love" only existed in Hollywood and romance novels. However, her way of thinking changed once Tyrese Whitman took her world by storm a year ago. Tyrese wined and dined her, and put to shame some of the best sex tales she ever read when they made love.

Tyrese was the kind of guy that could turn a woman to mush at the mere sight of him. One look in his eyes and a woman would imagine herself at the alter with him, and soon after 'I do' rushing off to a honeymooner's suite to do all sorts of things with him. He was just that sexy and alluring.

Last week, out of the blue, Tyrese popped the question, and Lela had been on cloud nine ever since. *Mrs. Lela Whitman,* she massaged the thought of being his wife into her mind, and thanked God for blessing her with a man. God knew she had her fair share of bad ones to last a lifetime.

Although he didn't keep a steady job, he was laying the groundwork to open an adult entertainment business. In the meantime, his only income came from hustling CD's and DVD's from his trunk, but the money coming into the house was little and far in between.

Consequently, Lela knew it wasn't about the money with Tyrese. He made her feel sexy, free, and safe with him. After her last lover from hell, Kelton Walker, stomped her heart into the ground, literally and figuratively, Tyrese was a breath of fresh air. He never raised his hand or voice at Lela, and as far as she could see, Tyrese was marriage material.

The only thing that irked her about him was his *"I'm not working for the white man"* mentality. If she had a dime for every time he said that, she would be richer than Bill Gates.

Though she could respect his ambitions to own his own business, that statement about drove her nuts! Sometimes a man has to swallow his pride and punch a clock for a paycheck while he is chasing his dreams. She constantly dropped subtle hints, hoping he would pick up on the fact that she needed him to bring home some steady money, especially since he promised to pay half the bills when he moved in months ago.

As long as he treated her like a queen and her six-year-old son, Antwan, like a prince, his being financially challenged did not stop her from accepting his love and reciprocating it.

When she thought back to her past relationships, she knew Tyrese treated her better than any of the other scrubs she had given her heart to. At the top of that scrub list was Kelton, who knew how to make a woman's life hang sideways. Even though Lela had broken up with Kelton two years ago, the painful memories from their relationship were etched into her psyche and set in stone, every terrifying moment.

To the average onlooker, Kelton and Lela had the picture-perfect relationship. He was a banker and she had a cozy job working from home. He had a daughter and she had a son. All of her family and friends lived their lives vicariously through Lela and Kelton. She drove the most expensive cars, dined at the most exquisite restaurants, and was showered with lavish gifts. All together, they were one big, happy, picture-perfect family.

That is, until their bedroom doors closed at night and Kelton unleashed the beast, using his fists to take out any frustrations he had on Lela. After beating her to a pulp, he would force her to satisfy him sexually, in anyway he wanted it. He was crazy like that. No one would have guessed "Angel-face Kelton" was so vicious, but Lela knew better.

One Saturday night, Lela's cousin, Trey, popped over to visit and see if Lela and Kelton wanted to hang out.

Not wanting Trey to see her bruised and swollen face, Lela hesitated with opening the door. But when Trey peeked through the blinds and playfully said, "I know you are in there, so open up," she reluctantly let him in.

She knew from the horrid look on his face that there was going to be trouble. "Trey, I'm fine. I fell and hit my face on the coffee table," she rushed to say. Lela laughed her injuries off as if they were miniscule.

When she saw that Trey wasn't falling for her façade, she said, "Just leave and come back later Trey. Just go, please!"

Ignoring her pleas, Trey barged through their house looking for Kelton. When he flew open the bedroom door, he found Kelton sitting on the bed with a crazed look on his face and an erection in his hand, ready for his post-beatdown sex.

"What the fuck—" is all Trey managed to say before he started wailing on Kelton's naked body. Trey struck Kelton with left hooks, right hooks, and jabs at what seemed to be lightening speed. Kelton didn't know what hit him. Hearing the commotion in the house, Trey's friend, Neil, who had been waiting outside in the car, came running inside and pulled Trey off of Kelton, who was now beaten to a pulp.

With Kelton slumped on the floor beside the bed, Trey told Lela to pack her things, and then took her and Antwan, who had been sleeping quietly in his bedroom on the other end of the house, to her mother's house. On the way to Miss Rachel's house, Neil consoled Lela, handing her tissue after tissue and telling her everything would be all right. Though it was the first time they met, Lela could appreciate genuine concern from him.

When Trey pulled in front of his aunt's house that night, his last words to Lela were, "I'm going to make sure that punk never puts his hands on you again. You just have to promise me you won't let him disrespect you like that ever again!"

Trey had always been very protective of Lela, but she did not want him to get himself hurt dealing with Kelton's craziness.

Lela willingly agreed through fearful lips not to go back under Kelton's abusive hand, and surprisingly enough, Kelton did not come after her like he had done on the rare occasions in the past when she had gotten the guts to flee from him.

To this day, whenever Lela saw Kelton limping around town, he would damn near trip over himself running the other way.

Fear is a mutha, ain' it, Kelton? Lela thought every time she saw the punk. She didn't know what Trey had done, but whatever it was it was one hundred percent effective in keeping Kelton away from her.

When she actually thought about it, none of her prior boyfriends treated her half as good as she treated them. She always gave one hundred percent and always got less than fifty percent in return.

Part 1

When A Good Thing Goes Bad

1
He's Mines

"I need to snap out of it and get moving!" Lela spoke to the emptiness of her bedroom. No matter how hard she tried to focus on her task at hand, like getting up and getting dressed for her girls' day out, she could not help but think back to last night.

Last night, she had been mentally exhausted after spending almost eight hours posted in front of her computer transcribing. When tantalizing smell made it hard for her to concentrate on work, she just knew she was imagining things. However, once she walked into her dining room, she was delighted to find that the delicious aroma was the real deal.

The table had been romantically set for two.

Lela's favorite meal, shrimp fried rice, prepared by none other than Chef Tyrese, was served on her crystal dinner plates and placed on her pedestal glass table. Her gold-tipped flute glasses, which she only used for special occasions, were half filled with white wine, and a bottle of Chardonnay rested in an ice bucket in the middle of the table.

"Mmmm. This smells delicious, babe! You did all of this for me? Thank you!" Lela beamed.

"No thanks necessary. I wanted to do something special for you. Besides, you've overworked your pretty little hands on the keyboard all day today and the only thing you are going to be using them the rest of the night for is pleasuring me. We have the house to ourselves for a change, and we are going to make good use of it...room by room."

Lela found herself blushing as she went to the sink to wash her hands. Usually, she and Antwan ate dinner together. Tyrese did not make it home until well after seven o'clock, and she would have his dinner waiting in the microwave. It was a refreshing change for Tyrese to have dinner laid out for her.

After dinner, Tyrese directed Lela to the bathroom while he washed the dishes. She smiled as she rushed to the bathroom to find rose petals and jasmine-scented bathwater awaiting her. Out of habit, she pushed the door closed behind her.

There on the door's hook hung a pink Victoria Secret bag adorned with a big white bow and a heart-shaped note. Inside, there was a red sexy *Babydoll* negligee and a large bottle of *Rapture*, her favorite perfume. Lela rushed to read the note: *"To the woman who lights up my life, forever and always. Love, Tyrese."*

Awe! But what is all of this for? And more importantly, where did he get money for this? She told herself to mask the cynicism and just enjoy the moment, but instinct got the best of her. "Last time I checked," she mumbled under her breath, "you were unemployed." The latter words resonated louder than she anticipated.

While her mind weighed the fact that Tyrese had not paid one bill this month, her body begged her to enjoy the sensational ride he was guaranteed to take her on -- if she could get past the pesky internal reminder that bills needed to be paid. Her mind, heart and body were in a constant struggle where Tyrese was concerned.

Just then, Tyrese waltzed proudly into the bathroom and placed one hand under Lela's chin, raising her face so that their eyes met. He kissed her passionately on her lush lips, allowing his colossal hand to seductively unbutton her shirt. "It's for you, babe. Just because."

I guess he overheard my mumbling. Well, there's no turning back now, Lela thought. It would have to be now or never to let him know that she'd rather have bill money than treats. "Because what, Ty? I need for you to...to help out..." Lela protested, though losing her effectiveness, "...more with the bills."

Instead of offering an answer, Tyrese kissed the softness between her breasts, taking a moment to suck on her jasmine-scented skin. Unsnapping her bra, he gently kissed her breasts giving them equal care and attention.

Once he worked Lela into a passionate frenzy, he leaned against the wall and licked his lips.

Tyrese standing there, licking his lips in all of his chocolate glory, brought Lela's protesting to a screeching halt. She had spent many days and hours massaging and adoring every tight muscle on his handsome body, and tonight would be no different.

"Oh, you are *good*, Ty. You are *too* good," she whispered as her hands wandered down to his zipper.

"Mmmm," he moaned in his best rendition of Barry White. Then, he took her pleasuring hand into his. "Not so fast. Tonight, we're taking things nice and slow."

He sat down on the toilet and began to explain the reason behind his romancing. "I've been hustling CD's and DVD's all day at Lamar's shop because I wanted to do something nice *for you* because you have been working so hard and holding me down. I just want you to know that you are appreciated.

"So soak your body, relax, and allow me to pamper you. Consider this night a token of my love for you. You can expect much more of this in the years to come, baby. *Today* is a new day." He gently guided her into the bubbles, and claimed her lips once again before slipping out of the bathroom.

Today is a new day. Lela didn't know exactly what he meant by the statement, but she liked the sound of it. For now, she settled on dropping the money subject.

After a relaxing bath, Lela applied lotion to her smooth, mocha latte skin and sprinkled edible powder evenly over her body. As she did a spin in the mirror, she noticed how the negligee fit perfectly over her curves. After heating her curling iron, she hit the ends of her silky wrap.

Entering the bedroom, she stood in awe at the scene before her. Several candles lined each side of her Manhattan style, queen-sized bed, creating a glow in the room. A silver serving tray with strawberries, whipped cream, melted chocolate, and two crystal wine glasses filled with the remainder of the Chardonnay sat on the nearby nightstand.

"Everything is so nice. I don't know what to say, Ty," Lela said as she slowly glided toward the bed.

"That's what I'm talking about! Show a brotha some love. But, be forewarned, I didn't do all of this to see what you would say," he hinted. "Now bring your sexy self on over here."

When Lela joined him underneath the sheets, she began to feed fresh strawberries dipped in melted chocolate into his hungry mouth. When he had his fill, she replaced the sweet fruit with her lip. She showed him no mercy as she savored every inch of his powerful frame.

After turning her onto her back and spreading her legs wide, Tyrese slid *deep* inside her inner core. She cried out in ecstasy as he rocked her world until the late hours of the night. He had her begging for mercy, only granting her wish when their aching muscles were too tired to move.

When the lovers were finally drifting off to sleep, Lela sent up a prayer. *Thank you, God, for sending me a decent man of my own.*

A twinge of guilt crept up her spine when she thought about the fact that what she had just done was fornication, so she adjusted her engagement ring on her finger and added, *and God please forgive me for my sins. We'll be married soon.*

After the breathtaking night Lela and Tyrese shared, Lela was all smiles when she was awakened by Tyrese showering kisses all over her neck as his strong hands caressed the warmth between her legs.

"I need to ask you something, babe," he whispered seductively.

Her eyes focused on the clock, which read 5:00 a.m.

"Anything, Ty," she murmured. At this moment, she was putty in his hands.

"Can I borrow three hundred dollars to get my alternator replaced?"

Lela figured she must have had a bothered look on her face when he quickly added, "Before you say anything, I will pay you back as soon as I sell my four-wheeler, babe. I just need to get my car fixed so I can have transportation to get out and make money for us. You know I'm always on the grind."

With it being her first time hearing about his car needing repairs, she was shocked to be hearing it now with his hand between her legs.

"You know I got you, Ty. I didn't know you were having problems with your car," she replied calmly, but deep inside, she was flipping out because by her giving him this money, it would mean she paid for her gifts yesterday *and* the dinner.

"Yeah, it started yesterday."

Lela pushed the covers back, climbed out of bed, found her wallet, and counted out three crisp one-hundred dollar bills, handing them to him. Even though she was tired of pulling the weight, she knew he was hustling to get his business off the ground, and she believed in standing by her man.

"Now, you said you would pay me back, right?"

He nodded his head. "Yes, of course...as soon as my four-wheeler sells."

While giving him a knowing grin, Lela glided back under the covers. "Well, come over here and finish what you started."

A few hours later was when the phone rang waking Lela from her deep slumber. She felt around in the tangled blankets, searching for the phone so she could put an end to its annoying shrill. She was pissed at whoever was responsible for pulling her out of her deep slumber.

"Hello," Lela answered groggily, not bothering to clear the sleep from her voice.

"Wake up, girl!" It was Tonya. "I'll be there in thirty minutes," Tonya sang.

Lela hated her friend for being so perky right now. Then she remembered what day it was. "Uh-uh, gimme like an hour."

Lela turned under the warmth of the comforters and focused on the red digital numbers of the tiny clock on her nightstand. *8:30 a.m.* It had barely been an hour since Tyrese left and she needed a little more time to recoup.

She heard Tonya suck her teeth and clear her throat. "I know you didn't forget," her friend said, and Lela could picture her rolling her eyes from the other end of the phone.

It was the first Saturday of the month, the day her and Tonya set aside for pampering and club hopping. Their day would consist of spa treatments and shopping and their night would be filled with booty shaking at whichever club was hitting.

"No!" Lela lied. "Damn, girl, I just got up." She didn't dare admit that she had pushed their plans to the back of her mind. Thanks to Tyrese, she had been floating high above the clouds since last night and didn't care to land anytime soon.

"Aiight, I'll be there in an hour. Be ready." Tonya sounded irritated.

"You just make sure you're here in an hour and don't have me waiting on you."

"Whatever sleepyhead."

Lela gently peeled back the red silk sheets entangling scantily clad body. Her pretty brown eyes instinctively fixated on the empty space beside her, a space only her beau could claim...Tyrese Whitman.

Tonya would be at her house within an hour honking her horn like a wild woman if she wasn't ready, so she knew she had to somehow pull herself together and get moving.

Thinking back to the time she shared with Tyrese before he left that morning had Lela in pure ecstasy. After getting out of bed, she placed the phone back in its cradle and hurried to get dressed.

As she danced into the bathroom, she thought, s*o what if I kick my man a few dollars. At least he's trying to get some business about himself so he can have a steady income. Plus, he's mine.*

2
Today is a New Day

Lela and Tonya had claimed the first Saturday of each month as their monthly holiday, L & T's Ladies' Day Excursion. As usual, their first stop was Golden Beauty Salon.

Lela's V-neck, rhinestone logo, South Pole hoodie allowed her breasts to nearly spill out of her shirt, causing every man she came in contact with to do a double take. When they passed Fred's Barbershop, two locally-known ballers, Mufassa and Contraband, came rushing out the door trying to push up on them.

"Ah, yo, yeah you...bring yo' fine ass back ova here," the tall dark-skinned brother sang out to Lela. The grill in his mouth was so big he could barely talk.

"What--ever!" Lela replied as she teased them with what they would never have by sashaying right on past the brothas. Her fitted rhinestone-designed blue-jean covered behind was a sure tease. She was about to marry the best thing Opelika had going for it, and there was nothing any other man could do for her.

Tonya, on the other hand, followed her friend's lead only because she knew the two men didn't make enough money to hold her attention. "Wannabes get on my last nerve," she told Lela, while flipping her long tresses over her shoulder and continuing her stride toward Golden Beauty Salon.

Since Tonya only needed her long, blond-streaked tresses curled, she was the first to get her hair done. In the meantime, Lela mulled over whether she would get a curly weave or wear her natural hair. The words Tyrese plunged into her soul with last night helped her quickly decide. *Today is a new day.*

"Give me a long curly weave, Quetta. I already washed it, so all you have to do is braid and stitch," Lela told her longtime beautician and friend after she had finished with Tonya's hair. She walked over to the case that held the different hair tracks. "I want this color."

"A weave? And with bronze highlights at that? What has gotten into my African Queen Au Naturale." Naquetta stood in shock that her friend had decided to go from a weekly hair pressing to a weave.

"Yes, girl, I'm ready for something new. Plus, you know I have to keep it hot for my 22-year-old fiancé." Lela raised her hand to show off her engagement ring once again. Naquetta had been one of the first people she told of her engagement last week.

"I heard that. Where is Tyrese's fine self anyway?"

"Girl, watch your mouth." Lela put her fist up and then laughed it off. They often teased each other about taking the other one's man. "He's getting his car fixed."

"That boy and his car."

"You know him well, don't you? He wouldn't survive a day without that car in working condition."

After three hours in Naquetta's chair, Lela's inner diva was born. Her curly tresses flowed down to her mid back and fit her pretty round face to perfection.

At the Colonial Mall, Lela and Tonya did some shopping. Lela was partial to a skirt and two shirts that Tonya picked out, but couldn't find anything she liked enough to buy for herself.

"I can't find anything I like. All of their stuff is so high," Lela said as she clinched her purse tightly to her side.

Sashaying around in her elegant, black, safari-style shirtdress and six-inch black stilettos, Tonya still would be a perfect dime even if she skipped out on the beauty treatments. Tonya could have passed for a supermodel..

"I know you're not going to be cheap today. You promised you would get jazzy with me tonight. How do you like these boots?" Tonya asked while strutting from one end of the Belk's dressing room to the other, as if she were modeling on a catwalk. "And let me tell you something," she warned Lela. "You better flaunt it while you got it, honey. One thing for sure is you'll never catch me half stepping."

"Whatever. You *need* to open a savings account, a checking account, a 401K, or something," Lela preached, and then digressed. "But don't let me get in the way of you trying to keep up with the

Joneses. Go on and get what you want. The boots are nice, but I'm going to Citi Trends."

"Stop it, I say! Unlike you, I'm not letting a 401K get all my money. I'll worry about retirement when I get there. I think I'm just going to chill on my fat social security check, anyway." Tonya laughed.

"Social security check? Girl, you're a trip. When you're old and broke, these hundred-dollar mini skirts aren't going to mean a thing." Lela laughed at the thought of an elderly Tonya switching around in a hot red mini skirt.

Ignoring Lela, Tonya winked and hissed at some fine brothers passing by, who did a U-turn and headed back their way.

"Well, right now, these mini skirts mean ballers like that are going to pay my way." Tonya rubbed her hands over the curve of her hips. "Hell, I'll get a man with a 401k and let him bank roll me when I'm sixty. I know if Grandma Jana's still reeling them in, I will have no problem." She then strutted over to some halter tops, as if what she spoke was the truth.

Lela shook her head. "What am I going to do with you *and* Grandma Jana?"

"Nothing, but love us." Tonya handed Lela a shirt with barely enough material to cover her upper assets. "Go try this on while I run some game down on these brothas and see where they pockets at."

After an hour of browsing and trying on different outfits, Lela settled on a Baby Phat ensemble, which consisted of a blue-jean pencil skirt and a sash tunic, all from the discount racks, of course. However, what she saved on the outfit she ended up splurging on a gorgeous pair of two-hundred-dollar Bijou pumps.

Tonya left the mall with about five bags in each hand, with a few of them compliments of one of the guys she whistled down earlier.

With shopping for their outfits out of the way, the next destination was the spa.

"I know you're going to let me spin the wheel this time. You told me you would let me drive your new whip, but I see you've been holding out with giving up the keys." As Lela reminded her friend, she stood by the driver's side of Tonya's brand new, black on black, 2005 Chrysler 300.

"Okay, but be gentle with my baby." Tonya tossed Lela the key, and they took off down Opelika Road.

"Oooooohhh! I've been craving ice cream all week. Before we go to the spa, I'm going to get me a butter-pecan cup from The Fat

Cherry in Tiger Village. You want one?" Lela asked over the sounds of her growling stomach. If anything was her weakness, butter-pecan ice cream and shrimp fried rice were the two things.

"Nah, I'm straight," Tonya replied. She was 5 feet 9 inches tall and weighed 140 pounds soaking wet. Yet, there was not a moment she didn't watch her weight.

Lela, on the other hand, was a generous 5 feet 4 inches and 165 pounds. She watched her weight and exercised, but did not have a problem with indulging in the finer foods in life. She didn't stress over her extra weight because most of it resided in her full breasts, luscious thighs, and voluptuous hips.

As they cruised down 280, heading toward The Fat Cherry, D4L's "Bet You Can't Do It Like Me" blasted through Tonya's Bose speakers. At the stoplight, they both sang and bounced to the latest southern group that had the south jumping off the map.

"Hey," Lela yelled over the music, "Ty bought me D4L's CD yesterday. So, now you can show me how to do the Laffy Taffy before we go out tonight. I want to know how to do it like the skinny light-skinned one. What's his name?"

Tonya searched her mind for the rap artist's name. "Who? Faybo? Girl, we need until next week for me to teach you to do it like that. You have to have skills like me to learn that fast." Tonya popped her shirt collar, boasting.

Lela hit her friend's shoulder playfully. "Whatever. Teach me anyway."

Out of the two of them, Tonya was the dancer. When they were kids, she was always coming up with dance routines for their dance group, the Spray Peppers, named after the female rap group Salt-N-Pepper. Tonya was Pepper, Lela was Salt, and Naquetta was Spinderella. You couldn't tell them that they weren't going to be superstars when they grew up.

Tonya made a mental note to bring Lela up on a few new dance moves before tonight since Lela was still stuck in the 1980's. The last time they went out, Lela took it upon herself to try to resurrect the Cabbage Patch. She had a crowd of mostly 20-year-olds weak from laughing at her old-fashioned dancing. Lela would take it back to the 80's in a heartbeat, and had no shame in her game.

"Aiiight," Tonya replied, giving in. "Good thing you got me as a friend, girl," she added while turning down the music. "Leave it up to you, and you'll be doing the Running Man, with no one to tell you that it's not cool."

"You know me well," Lela laughed while turning the music back up.

The stoplight had turned green, but Lela did not go. Something in her right field of vision had her full attention. Before she could formulate words to speak, Tonya read her mind.

"Is that Tyrese's car?"

"Yeah, but I thought he would still be at the auto shop," Lela said with a tinge of suspicion.

Parked directly in front of The Fat Cherry, his car was hard to miss. He drove the only Caprice in town that was a rolling advertisement for the Auburn Tigers football team. The car had orange candy paint with a blue leather interior. In big blue letters, TYRESE was spelled out on the trunk. To match his car, most days he would be dressed down to the socks in Auburn University paraphernalia.

Lela swooped into the parking lot and parked directly in front of his car.

"That's his car alright, and look-a-here."

3

The Fat Cherry

The Fat Cherry was bizarrely packed this early afternoon. Guilt and uneasiness crept up Tyrese's spine when Sarah dipped a cherry into her banana split and fed it to him, letting her syrupy-sweet finger linger on his tongue a little too long.

He was apprehensive about taking Sarah to The Fat Cherry in the first place, but she was adamant, saying, "Come on, Ty. It has my favorite dessert, other than you."

Now, he was sitting in a corner booth with Sarah, licking his lips in a LL Cool J type of way and trying to figure an escape out of this mess. Truth be told, he had been ready to leave as soon as they got there. Being seen in public with Sarah was the last thing he wanted or needed, especially today when it seemed like everyone was out. He had been very careful to keep their relationship on the low, and their intimacy had been primarily confined within the walls of her apartment.

Making an attempt at escape, he whispered seductively in her ear. He caressed her creamy, pale thighs and found what he was looking for, allowing his fingers to work their magic. "Sarah, let's go back to your place. I'm ready to get to the real dessert, your fat red cherry."

As expected, she went into a sex haze, repaying his touch with caresses of her own. Her flushed cheeks gave him hope that his strategy was working. She seemed to be oblivious to the fact that he was more interested in getting out of public with her than getting into her panties.

Ty knew he had her melting, literally, in his hands when she stared deep into his eyes and blushed uncontrollably. He flashed his bedroom smile, hoping she would speed their so-called date up. However, when she pulled herself out of the lustful daze, Tyrese knew he was in trouble.

"Ty, you promised to take me shopping. All we ever do is get our freak on in my apartment. I'm starting to think you are ashamed of me or something."

There she goes again. Always thinking I'm ashamed of our interracial relationship. He should have seen that one coming. Even though the Deep South had taken many positive strides forward, he could not refute the fact that hostile stares were routine whenever he took her out, which was a rarity. Afterwards, Tyrese always shied away from her. Even this afternoon at The Fat Cherry, he caught a few eyes glowering in their direction.

Now, Sarah was on to his game that he was using sex to lure her back to her apartment. Little did he know, though, Sarah had made a pact with herself today. She and Ty would not run and hide. Instead, he would follow through with his promise to take her out shopping today. She planned on spending some of that money he always bragged about.

"Okay, baby girl," he said, "I did promise." He tried to remember precisely what the hell he was thinking about when he made that stupid promise. Then it came to him. *It was Thursday night when I was knee deep in the punani, promising to give her any and everything she wanted.* He could kick himself for letting sex drive him to the point of promising his mistress a date. Nevertheless, here he was.

He made a mental note to never get caught up like that again. Living in a small city, he never knew who he would bump into.

Eager to abort this impromptu outing, Tyrese licked his lips with a formula designed only for him, and said, "Come on then, baby girl. What do you want to do first?"

"Let's go to the mall."

"Good. I'll take her to the Peachtree in Columbus." He decided moving their date to another city would be his best bet.

At that very moment, Tyrese felt an eerie presence surrounding him that he could not shake. The feeling was unsettling to the third power. His heart fluttered as he took a brief look around the restaurant. Seeing that the coast was clear, he stood to help Sarah from her seat.

4

Cold Busted

L ela's long-lashed brown eyes did a double take. She did not want to believe what she saw. Her man's arm was snugly wrapped around some white chick.

"I know he's not out here advertising this...this bitch," Lela yelled, with more disappointment than anger, but it was not long before anger took up residence in every bone in her body. By this time, Lela was out of the car and moving full speed, with her beautiful black weave dancing in the wind. She was at The Fat Cherry's glass door before Tonya knew she had even exited the car.

"Wait, Lela!" Tonya tried unsuccessfully to stop her. She knew with Lela's temper anything was possible, and she was not about to let her girl scrap without her. So, she took off her stilettos and earrings and followed behind Lela.

Lela's eyes confirmed what her heart wanted to deny. Tyrese was all over some high-priced, model-looking white girl. He was devouring the girl's hot fudge-covered finger like it was the best thing since sliced bread. "Hell to the naw!" she screamed while still standing outside The Fat Cherry. She lingered at the establishment's glass door, committing the scene in front of her to memory.

Entering the store, she moved like a stealth assassin in Tyrese's direction. He appeared to be so into his date, he didn't notice Lela or Tonya approaching their table.

Lela's rule of thumb in the past had been to never blame the woman, but she had a good mind to beat the girl down on sheer principle. She hadn't quite decided what she was going to do to Tyrese yet.

Unaware of their plight, Tyrese and Sarah giggled and flirted seductively back and forth.

Lela came completely unglued when she heard him say, "Come on then, baby girl. What do you want to do first?" and she responded, "Let's go to the mall."

When Tyrese rose to help his date from her seat, he turned and found himself standing face to face with Lela. He quickly gave Sarah an order, but kept his eyes glued to Lela.

"Go on to the car, Sarah." His voice was low and controlled. "I got to take care of something."

Sarah looked from Lela to Tyrese, then from Tyrese to Lela. "What's the problem, babe?"

That's when Lela took it back to 1999. "Bitch, you the problem! You got some nerve sitting up here with my man asking questions." By now, she was all in Sarah's face. "And if you don't keep it moving, you about to find out exactly how big the problem is!" Lela turned to Tyrese. Now it was his turn for a reading. "And you, Ty! Are you forgetting that I paid for that damn car, the same one you are sending her out to? How could you do some shit like this?"

"That's right. This negro done lost his damn mind!" Tonya chimed in from her friend's side. She looked more pissed off than Lela.

Tyrese stood there like a deer caught in headlights. His silence only added fuel to Lela's fire. "You don't have nothing to say?"

Sarah, who ignored her orders to go to the car, stood by her man. She gave Lela a look to show she wasn't no punk about hers either.

"Who is this woman, Ty?" Sarah asked with attitude.

Lela sized up the opponent. She noticed one high-end piece of clothing on top of another covering her gorgeous skin. Sarah had twists in the front of her hair and beautiful, blonde, ringlet curls adorning her perfect long neck. If Sarah came at her wrong, Lela's first move would be to get a vice grip on the hair at the nape of her neck and bang her head into the table.

"I'm his fiancée," Lela replied with just as much attitude. "And I'm the one he has to answer to, not you."

"Damn straight!" Tonya added.

Sarah shot Lela and Tonya an unaffected look. "Fiancée? What a joke. Toss me the keys, Ty." She laughed like Katt Williams had just walked out on to an imaginary stage or something. "Oh, and babe," she purred at Tyrese while flipping her shoulder-length hair from one side to the other, "don't make me wait too long."

Her words along with her actions set Lela's temperament to boiling, causing Lela to lunge at her. Ty caught her fist inches away from Sarah's rosy cheeks. "You gonna be waiting on an ambulance if you don't get outta here! Let me go, Ty!" Lela ordered.

In a rush to keep Sarah from ending up in the ER, Ty reached in his pocket, and then tossed Sarah his car keys.

"I hope this doesn't mess up my shopping trip," Sarah told Tyrese with her nose in the air. At the door, Sarah gave Lela one final "Oh…and he's *our* man" look.

Lela used everything in her power to keep her composure, though her spirit was broken. Hurt as she was, she was not about to be a crying fool in public, and especially not in front of Tonya who was now following Sarah out the door.

And this is where he proposed to me, Lela cried on the inside. She held her ring finger up to meet his eyes. A diamond and gold engagement ring sparkled there. He had given it to her only one week prior. It was not much, but she had been proud to wear it.

"Did this ring mean anything to you, Ty?" Lela's voice was barely above a whisper.

He opened his mouth, but she raised her hand to cut off whatever variation of the truth he would attempt to come out the bag with. She would not allow him to sugarcoat the situation this time, as he had done so many times before.

"What do you think you are doing? I mean...really." She took a look around. "I have to say this is a nice place for a date, but have you no shame?"

Confusion consumed him as he tried to figure a way out of this mess. When he didn't respond, Lela continued her tongue lashing.

"One week…just one week ago you proposed to me. Then, the next week, you're out here about to suck another woman's finger off her hand—in the same place and even the same booth." She waved her hands over the scene. "At least you treat all your women equal," she said sarcastically. " What's your plan, to keep me around long enough to get your business off the ground and then leave me for your white girlfriend? Let me guess. You expect me to suck it up and be the butt end of this joke, huh?"

Tyrese attempted to take her hand in his, but she snatched her hand away with such force that he shook. He opened his mouth, but only air came out.

"Don't you ever touch me again!" Lela shouted. "Touch that bitch!" She pointed toward his car, where his date had disappeared to.

"She's a friend. That's all, Lee," he finally found his voice to speak.

She smirked. "You take me for a special kind of fool, don't you? However, this is crystal clear. In my heart of hearts, I knew you'd been playing me, but I always gave you the benefit of the doubt. I believed what you told me. But, now that I've walked up and touched you, playa, let's keep it simple."

He reached for her again, still trying to think of a way to explain himself.

"Ty, life is too short for this mess. The only reason I came in here–and interrupted you and your snow bunny–was so you could not squirm your way out of the truth."

Lela glanced around and saw they now had an alarmed audience. She knew the Opelika PD would be on the scene soon, so she brushed by Tyrese and headed to the car. "You know what? I'm out of here."

Before exiting The Fat Cherry's doors, she whipped around and added, "For all intents and purposes, Ty, we are through. Your stuff will be on the lawn by the time you drop your date off at home."

She started to walk away again when a tiny voice in her head stopped her in her tracks. It was the voice of her mother, saying, "If you let somebody screw you once, shame on them. If you let somebody screw you twice, shame on you."

She remembered she had loaned Tyrese three hundred dollars to get his car fixed, and she would be damned if he flossed around town spending her money on another woman. He left her house that morning headed to the auto shop; yet, his car was miraculously in mint condition and he was out on a date. Just when she was about to address this, he attempted to pacify her, making his first real attempt at recovery.

"Calm down, babe. It's not what you think. I don't give a damn about Sarah. I love you."

With each word he spoke, Lela felt her walls of defense slowly melting away.

"So you're loving *me* now, Ty? Well, you can save it and give it to your precious little girlfriend." Lela fought feelings of hurt and shame, still determined not to cry. "If you *loved* me so much," she continued, "you wouldn't be out here spending my hard-earned money like this. And I know you're using my money, so don't even try to lie."

"I did need the muffler," he blurted out. "I got it."

"Muffler? I thought it was an alternator you needed." She threw her hands in the air. "You know what? I don't care what it was. Give me my money. Now! And give me the keys to my house and the spare keys you have to my Jeep." She pointed to Sarah, who was sitting on the passenger side of his car filing her fingernails. "You're her dependent now."

"I don't have the money, Lee. I already ordered the muff...I mean, alternator." He would ride or die with this lie.

"Look, Ty, give me my money." Lela didn't know what she was capable of doing next if she didn't get what she felt he owed her.

Taking her by surprise, he forcefully wrapped his arms around her waist. "Calm down, babe. I told you this girl is just a friend of mine. It's not even like that. She has connections in the movie industry and I'm using her to help get my business started," he lied. "I'll be home when you get there; so there is no need for you to be taking the keys and stuff. We can talk about this then."

Lela forcefully pushed him off of her. "Talk? You must have me confused with the next female. All we got to talk about is my money, and we're doing that now." She tapped her nails together, motioning for him to place the money and keys in her hand.

When she looked into his eyes, she felt not an ounce of love for Tyrese. She didn't know what was sucking the love out of her more: catching him with another female, or seeing him for the first time as the leech that he was. The fact that he thought they could go back to life as usual after her catching him red-handed would have been funny if he hadn't looked so stupid saying it.

Tyrese suddenly became irritated. "I see why Kelton used to go upside your head. You're so temperamental. You don't understand the struggles of the black man. Sometimes, we got to be chummy with these white folks to get what we want out of life. She is helping me break into the entertainment business." He was in a mode Lela had never seen him in. Towering over her, he added, "I'll give you the money and keys, but I got to get my stuff out your house first before I give you anything. Now go home and I'll be there in a minute."

"So now the truth comes out. You think you know why Kelton

used to 'go upside my head.' Well, if you don't give me my money, you're going to find out how Kelton got that limp of his." Lela was yelling at the top of her lungs when Tonya walked back in from the parking lot, where she had been trying to pick a fight with Sarah.

"Come on, Lela," Tonya urged.

"I'm coming when I get my stuff," Lela shouted.

Tonya grimaced, then taking note of the unusually still scene around them, she made Lela aware of it, as well. "Uh, Lela, take a look around."

Lela scanned The Fat Cherry. Everyone was dead silent. Some had even stopped eating. She softened her tone of voice, but still made herself clear to Tyrese.

"The locks will be changed and your stuff will be in a nice little bonfire in the backyard by the time you get your Barbie home, Ty. So try me, and you'll regret it."

Tyrese looked at Sarah, who was still outside, then back at his fiancée.

Lela felt her disgust-o-meter rise ten levels when he checked up on his lover who was sitting nonchalantly in the car, filing her nails. The same car she had paid for. She realized she would have to charge the car to the game since she had been stupid enough to put the title in his name.

She pushed a strand of her jet-black curly weave away from her face. Even seven years his senior, she emitted beauty from her head down to her French-pedicured toes. She was not anyone's second pickings by any stretch of the imagination, and it was time Tyrese learned what toast tasted like without her butter.

Ty walked out of The Fat Cherry with Lela and Tonya right behind him. He went straight to his freshly detailed Chevy Caprice. Thanks to Lela, it was sitting on 22-inch chrome wheels. He opened the passenger's door while Lela and Sarah watched his every move. He then reached over Sarah's lap, unlocked the glove compartment, and pulled out a fat envelope. He handed Lela three crisp one-hundred-dollar bills and removed her house keys and spare jeep keys from his keychain, handing them to her, also.

With attitude, Lela snatched her money and keys from his hand. As she got into the passenger side of Tonya's car, she yelled, "I'll have your clothes ready for you in the driveway."

★ ★ ★

After Lela and Tonya pulled off, Tyrese handed Sarah a dollar. "Catch the bus home," he said with urgency. "I'll hit you up later."

"What?" Sarah asked, certain she had heard him wrong.

"You know my crazy baby momma I been telling you about?" he lied.

"Yeah."

"Well, that's her."

"She said she was your fiancée, Ty. And what was that about her having your clothes ready?"

"I told you she was crazy. She's always saying stuff like that just to run off any girl I'm with. She knew when she saw you I had a good thing. I told her I was feeling you."

Before kissing Sarah's forehead, Ty made sure Lela was nowhere in sight.

"Look, she was just flipping out because I forgot it was my weekend to pick up my daughter. I need to get over to her mom's place ASAP so her mother can go to work."

"I still don't see why you can't at least take me home."

Once again, Tyrese would ride or die with a lie. "She's threatening to take away my visitation *and* go up on my child support if I don't get there before she does. And you know how important my daughter is to me."

As far as Sarah knew, Tyrese was the VP of Operations at Auburn Urgent Hospital, so she could see why the mother of his child would threaten to get more child support.

"Alright, but this *won't* happen again." She rolled her eyes as she gathered her belongings from the floor of his car.

"Oh, I promise to make it up to you."

Sarah smiled. "I can think of some ways you can do that. But you know you can't let her dictate your life like this...*our* lives like this."

"Yeah, I know," Tyrese shot back as he peeled out of the parking lot.

5

Operator this is An Emergency

T yrese was accustomed to getting what he wanted…the way he wanted…*anytime* he wanted it from her, so the fact that his car was in its usual parking space in Lela's driveway when Tonya dropped her off didn't come as a surprise.

"He must have dumped ole girl off on the highway or something. Do you need me to come in with you?" Tonya unsnapped her seatbelt and popped her knuckles like a soldier ready for combat.

"No, I got this girl. You go on, and I'll call you later."

"Lela, don't you dare think about letting this slide. He was out on a date. Your eyes didn't deceive you. Ty is full of it, and you know it."

"Don't you worry about me. I will make sure Tyrese gets his."

"See, that's what I'm worried about."

On the walk up the driveway, Lela thought back a few months to when she flew out to California to visit Grandma Jana.

She and Grandma Jana had a blast. They went shopping, hung out, and Grandma Jana schooled Lela on how to get and keep a man. By Saturday, Lela missed Tyrese so much she rushed home a day early.

"Ty!" she called out as she burst through the front door of her house. She knew he was there; his car was in the driveway. "Ty, baby, I'm home!"

She almost tripped over beer bottles strewn throughout the house. The stinking smell of Coors almost made her gag, but she still was anxious to see her man. Rushing to the bedroom, she found Ty in bed snoring, his naked body tangled in her red satin sheets. The room stank with a whiff of something she didn't want to recognize.

Lela kissed him on the cheek, ignoring his bad breath and unshaved face. She shook her head. *Look how pitiful he looks. He must have missed me.*

Since he would not wake up, Lela decided to clean up around the house a little bit. When she picked up Ty's clothes, which she later discovered he wore out to the club the night before, she thought her heart had been ripped out of her chest after an empty condom packet fell to the floor.

Later that night, Ty finally woke up from his drunken slumber and gave Lela a convincing story. "It was Sydney's. I found the condom wrapper on the floor when I got home from the club last night. So, you know, I called Sydney right then because he was the only one over here yesterday...and he was like 'yeah, I boned Teresa on the couch while you were in the shower.'"

Ty continued to explain, hoping she would believe his concocted tale. "Then I picked the wrapper up, planning to put it in the trash, but put it in my pocket instead. I don't know, man...I was too tight off that Grey Goose to even think straight."

Seeing that his story was going over remarkably well with Lela, he continued with one eyebrow raised. "Do you really think I would be that sloppy to leave the wrapper right here in the floor, baby? Do you really think that little of me?"

Just like that, the game was reversed. Lela was on the defensive about a condom wrapper that fell out of *his* pocket. Teresa was her hoochie mama neighbor and Sydney would bone anything with a snatch and two legs, so his story was convincing enough. She remembered feeling like a fool for questioning Tyrese. Now, her better judgment told her that he cheated on her. An old saying came to mind: *If it acts like a...looks like a...it might be a...*

But, Lela refused to be played this time.

On the ride home from The Fat Cherry, she did a little scheming of her own. She knew just how to pay Tyrese back if he was stupid enough to be at her house when she got there. Just like she thought, he used her spare key under the flowerpot to gain entrance.

When Lela stepped into her foyer, Ty pulled her into a tight hug. "Baby, I'm sorry. I know you're mad right now, and you have a right to be. I'll do whatever it takes, for however long it takes, to make this up to you. I don't care about that girl. You mean everything to me. I really meant it when I said I love you, and I want you to be my wife. You mean the world to me. It will never happen again. Never."

"You got that right." She knew one thing for sure and two things for certain. One, this would never happen again. Two, he was surely a sorry-ass excuse for a man.

With her plan in mind, she kept quiet and let him do all the talking.

He didn't waste time turning on his charm like a light switch. She fell for his wooing...or so he thought...and allowed Ty to take her into the bedroom and give his best attempt at making up. She seriously considered forgiving and forgetting, but the image of Tyrese, the white girl, and their romantic encounter kept playing out in her head–even as she took pleasure in what he was doing to her body. Lying on her back, looking into the depth of his eyes as he plunged deeper and deeper inside her, she ran the pains and pleasures of the moment down in her head.

Look at him, she thought. *Pathetic! Mmmm...that feels sooooooooo good...He has the nerve to look at me the same way he did her no less than an hour ago...Yeah, right there, oh yeah...If he can get out of my bed after a night like we had last night, and then go take his other woman out, then there's nothing else I can do to keep him from straying again...I hate your fine ass with that damn ripped body. And ooooohhh, I'm going to miss this you babe. Uhhhhh, I'm coming... It's going to be hard to let go.* By this time hot tears flowed freely down her face. She raged, cried and released all at the same time.

Pulling her sweaty, throbbing body from underneath Tyrese, Lela headed to the shower.

"Where are you going?"

"To take a shower. I've got to wash your funky sweat off me," she lied. The intoxicating aroma from his Dolce & Gabanna cologne could have lingered on her for a lifetime...before today.

Thirty minutes later, Lela emerged from the master bathroom with her terry robe tied snugly around her waist. She picked up the phone, dialed some numbers, and then sat down on the edge of the bed as she applied lotion to her legs.

"Hey. We still on for tonight?" Lela asked as she kept her sad, brown eyes affixed to Ty, who just knew he was the man-twenty-grand after putting it down like a pro.

Lela wanted to make sure he knew he was still kicked to the curb, so she made sure he overheard her phone conversation loud and clear. "Tonya," Lela grinned, "I'm ready to get my party on and celebrate the fact that I'm a free woman."

Lela shot Tyrese a nasty look as she spoke to Tonya, while holding the phone to her ear with her shoulder and applying the lotion with her free hands. Her mood change caused him to look at her sideways.

Usually his lovemaking had Lela ready to cosign her name for anything he wanted or needed. So his pride made him clueless. He rolled out of bed and walked into the kitchen, never noticing that for the first time in the past week Lela's ring finger was bare.

Lela knew it was time to put the nail in the coffin when he strutted back in her bedroom with his chest stuck out like a man worth a million bucks. In three large gulps, he downed the bottle of water he got from the refrigerator, then claimed his spot in bed beside Lela and rubbed her thighs.

"Girl, you know you love this king ding-a-ling, so stop tripping and come over here and get you some more of this. If anything I know about my baby, it's that she's a closet freak."

Jerk. Lela rolled her eyes so hard, she thought they were going to pop out of their sockets. Picking the phone back up from its cradle, she dialed the magic numbers.

"This is 9-1-1. What is your emergency?"

Lela looked at Tyrese with his happy-go-lucky self. His confidence got on her last nerve, but this would be his wake-up call. It was time to unleash the drama queen, and she knew exactly how to bring her out.

"Operator!" she screamed, "I'm hurt bad! There's a man here in my house! Please, I want him out!" Her voice flipped to high-pitched and hysterical. "He beat me! Hurry, I don't know what he'll do next!"

If Tyrese was looking at her sideways before, the mixture of confusion and fear he had on his face then took crazy to the next level. Jumping to his feet, he said, "What are you doing? Why are you calling the police?"

She raised her right hand in a "talk to the hand" motion as she smiled into the phone. She ignored him as she panted into the phone like a woman in distress.

The supportive operator asked her to provide more information, including the name of the assailant.

"Tyrese Whitman!" She told the operator. "My ex-boyfriend. He just jumped on me and won't leave." She panted hysterically.

His crazed look could have pierced her skin when she said his name. One thing about Tyrese, he was terrified of the police. He'd just as soon take off running the other way than walk past a police officer on the sidewalk, so she knew he would punk out if she called them to the house.

The operator then asked if the assailant was on the lease.

"No, I'm the only one on this mortgage. He is an intruder!" Then she thought to herself, *Thank God I don't have his name on anything in my house, because the police would not be able to remove him from the premises.*

Then Lela heard exactly what she wanted to hear.

"We're sending an officer out right now, ma'am."

"Thank you! You might be saving my life!"

After Lela disconnected the call, Tyrese shot all up in her face, demanding answers.

"What the hell have you just done?" he yelled.

She glared at him like a tiger going in for the kill, and then laid into him. "Don't act stupid! But, just in case it is not an act, let me spell it out for you. If you were stupid enough to think things were just going to fall back into place because we had sex, then you're even more washed up than I thought you were. Now, get out of here with a quickness, and don't leave anything behind or it will be trashed."

Tyrese was at a loss for words. "But, Lela, you didn't have to...we just finished...we coulda...I woulda...you shoulda..."

"It's a little late for coulda, woulda, shoulda. You coulda, woulda, shoulda thought about how I would feel when I walked in on you cheating on me. If you don't want to deal with the Opelika PD, I suggest you just get out. You can get your white woman, what's her name–Tara, Sarah–to carry your heavy load from now on." She laughed. "Oh, and thanks for tightening a sistah up one more time for the road. I really appreciate that, *brah*." She had to show some guts now, she could cry later.

From a distance, police sirens were blaring, but not yet in front of the house.

As a teen thug wannabe in Newnan, Tyrese had his share of unpleasant run-ins with redneck cops. Scurrying around her house, he grabbed his belongings as quickly as he could.

"You wrong for this, Lela! This is foul, man!" Tyrese had the role of victim down pat. He really couldn't believe she would treat him so cold.

"No, *you* wrong for this! I have done nothing but be good to you ever since we have been together...even when I knew some of the things you were doing were shifty."

"But we can work this out..."

"You should have been worrying about *working* and home while you were out broadcasting your other woman all over town. This is the end of the road, Ty, and I'm not going to sit here and waste any more of my breath on you."

Adamant on staying clear of the police, Tyrese ran out the front door. With his duffle bag draped across his back, he ran out of her life as quickly as he had run in.

Proud that she had the strength to send him packing, Lela got up, then locked and latched the door behind him, sealing closed this saga of her heart.

Looking around at her empty home, she already missed the security of having a man there. She would miss their long talks about everything and nothing. She would definitely miss his warm hugs and hot touches in places that made her blush, which is why she couldn't resist one last sensual ride before she issued his walking papers.

Deep down, she knew this wasn't the first time Tyrese had cheated, but a man spending *her* money on *another woman* was definitely not something Lela wanted to get used to.

6
Good News, Bad News

"Larna! Come here, babe. I got some good news. I got *good* news. Put on your dancing shoes, sweetheart," Neil called out as soon as he closed the front door to his Victorian-style home. "You won't believe what happened to me at the office today."

Neil removed his tie and blue button-up shirt, then grabbed two champagne glasses out of the cabinet and a bottle of Moet from the icebox. Making his way to the master bedroom, he could not wait to tell his girlfriend that he had been promoted to vice president.

When he heard the soft music playing from behind the closed bedroom door, he smiled. That could only mean one thing. Larna was soaking in some sweet smelling bubbles and would be just right for him to make love to her. At that moment, Neil was definitely glad to be in his skin.

His body stiffened in anticipation as the sounds of Sons of Funk's "Pushin' Inside of You" cascaded softly through his bedroom door.

He removed his white undershirt, black slacks and socks, and plaid boxers, and left them in the hall as he entered the room with nothing but the champagne bottle and glasses. He called out to her softly. "Larna..."

The sound of glass breaking caused Larna to jump up from the bedroom sofa.

"Cornelius! Babe, what are you doing home so early? I thought you called and said you would be working late. *Why* did you come home so early?" She was talking a mile a minute. "I didn't want you to find out like this."

"What...what the hell is going on here?" Neil could not hide hurt in his low, cracking voice.

His first instinct was to throw hands with the person who had been stroking his woman with the biggest, blackest dildo he'd ever seen. The size of the dildo sent a wave of intimidation over Neil causing his disposition to change from hurt to horror. He had an above-average package himself, but he had never imagined competing with a mechanism of that magnitude.

He quickly remembered his own nakedness, so he stormed back into the hallway and put on his boxers. The last thing he wanted was to be tussling with another butt naked individual.

Larna and her lover followed suit, putting on as many clothes as they could before Neil came back in.

"Don't worry, babe," Neil heard Larna's accomplice say. "You can always come home with me. I told you before that I'll take care of you better than he can. You don't need this buster."

Neil was hearing Cindy assert a manliness that she obviously only exerted behind closed doors. With a large chip on his shoulder, Neil barged back into the room. It had not been long ago that he had been dodging Cindy's sexual advances.

"You two nasty tricks! Get out of my house!" Neil stood in shock and awe that his girl's best friend had been laying more pipe in her than he ever could.

As Cindy tossed the two-headed dildo onto the bed and scrambled to put the rest of her clothes on, Larna tried desperately to explain. "No, I don't want to leave. We need to talk...Neil baby, please listen to me." Afraid her pleas were falling on deaf ears, she went to the heart of the matter. "You were never here. I needed someone, and Cindy was always here for me." And as if it would make things better, Larna added, "At least I didn't cheat with a man. Baby, this is not even really cheating."

Neil looked at the two ladies and, for a brief second, thought maybe the three of them could work something out. It had been his fantasy to be with two women, but it didn't take long for that idea to pass. Just thinking about Cindy plunging that 14-inch apparatus in and out of what he considered *his* was just not right.

"To hell, you say, it's not cheating! It is what it is, Larna. Now, don't let me get in the way of you and your *wo*man. You all just need to find some other place to handle your business."

He could not believe she had the nerve to be sprawled out on his newly imported plush leather sofa -- that she helped him pick out -- getting it on, with her best friend to boot. The more he thought about it, the more irate he became. "Get out now!"

Since Larna would not take the initiative to leave on her own, Neil rummaged through the drawers as quickly as he could and emptied out her stuff. "Take it now, because this is the last you will see of this place."

Under any other circumstance, he probably would have jumped in the bed feeling happier than a sissy with a bag full of dicks with these two beautiful bi-sexual women. Larna was 5'9" with a slim waist and the best set of artificial tits money could buy. Cindy had pouty lips that beckoned to suck something, and Neil always thought she had a nice butt, but without her clothes, it seemed to be double the size. It just so happened that he cared about Larna, and the pain of finding her cheating on him in the home they shared was devastating.

He had thought Larna was wife material. She was drop dead gorgeous, cooked and cleaned and they had mind-blowing sex, but best of all she could hold up her end of a mentally stimulating conversation. He had even visited his jeweler a couple times in the last few weeks thinking *one day* he would make an honest woman out of her and marry her.

Now, he was glad he didn't buy a ring as he looked at Larna standing in his bedroom with Cindy, her dirty little secret. He regretted every dime and every bit of energy he had spent on her.

Defeated, Larna walked past him with her last bag and said, "Neil. Just know that I loved you...but...but...you were never here."

Neil didn't dare look up at her for fear she would see his bloodshot eyes. "Just go."

It was true that he was never home, but Neil needed someone who had the will to hang in there with him through the rough times as he climbed the ladder at Naytek.

Later that evening, he called Trey. "You won't believe the mess I've been through today. Let's go out tonight and get into something and I'll explain it to you then."

$$\frac{7}{}$$
We Be Clubbin'

After calling her mother's house and talking to Antwan, Lela spent half the afternoon holed up in her bedroom, sipping Camelot and shedding tears. She had put up a bold front when she threw Ty out, but the thought of being alone again frightened her. Knowing she had Antwan to be strong for was the only thing that kept her from slipping deeper into her depression.

Tonya came back a few hours later to check on her friend and found her moping around the house.

"You know what?" Tonya consoled her friend. "You are smart, sexy, and best of all, you are my girl. So you know that means you have something going for yourself. Trust, I would not be hanging around you if you were busted. I always knew you could do better, Lela, and now is your chance to prove it to yourself. "

"Now you tell me I could do better," Lela said nonchalantly while pouring herself another glass of the soothing red liquid.

"Yes. Now, I'm telling you, and you know you would not have listened to me as long as you thought Tyrese could do no wrong. Some lessons are better learned by trial and error. If you think about it, I have been on you all along about giving him money, a car, and clothes, when the damn fool didn't even have the decency to go apply for work. But, that's all water under the bridge now."

"Yeah, water under the bridge." Lela downed the rest of the drink in her glass and poured another. "I'm still going out tonight, but I don't know how much fun I'll be." She blew her nose into a tissue as she searched her mind for ways to satisfy her shattered heart. *A new man?* She tossed out the idea as soon as it entered her thoughts. *The last thing I need is to be on the rebound at a dang-on nightclub, of all places. All that will mean is the same problem with a different person. Damn you, Ty!*

The ladies looked through Lela's closet, searching for something to wear. When Lela spotted the polo dress Ty had bought for her, a lone tear slipped from the corner of her puffy eyes. She remembered him bringing it home with a super-sized teddy bear for her birthday three months ago. She pushed the dress to the back of the closet and took her Baby Phat outfit, which she bought earlier that day, off its hanger and placed it on the bed.

The twenty-minute ride to The Foxy Lady from Lela's house was quiet.

Pulling into the parking lot, Tonya asked Lela, "Is Pastor Leroy here tonight or something?" The rapper was notorious for popping in at this club.

There were so many cars in The Foxy Lady's parking lot, the ladies contemplated leaving. "It looks like they are packed tight. Do you think we're going to be able to get in?" Lela asked, with a sparkle of hope that she would make it back to her bedroom to the wine and tissues that were calling for her.

"Lela, I know we can get in. Look who's working the door." It was Spanky, Lela's old boyfriend. Lela was in a catch twenty-two. On the upside, Spanky was still putty in her hands, even though they had not dated in years. On the downside, he was relentless with his macking. He took it to the point of aggravation.

"We might even get in VIP tonight if you show him a little interest. Come on; let's go to the front of the line."

A prominent male's voice stopped Lela in her tracks. "Little cuz, I know you're not going to walk past me without hollering at your boy."

"Heeeeyyy, Trey." Lela's sad cheeks turned up into a big smile as she ran over to her cousin, hugging him tightly around his back. "How you been, boy? I haven't seen you in so long. I know you are going to get your girl in, VIP style."

"Yeah, come on." He turned and told the people behind him in line, "These ladies are with me."

"So how are Uncle Calvin and Aunt Dawn?" Calvin was her mother's brother.

"Daddy is doing his thing, as usual. Always trying to find new DJ gigs. And Aunt Dawn is doing her thing. She might be up in the club. Anyway, you should go see them sometimes because Momma is always asking about you." That news made Lela smile since Dawn was her favorite aunt.

"Hey, Tonya," Trey said, acknowledging Lela's friend.

"Hi." Tonya adjusted her black skirt, then positioned and repositioned her pink V-neck chiffon top. She rubbed her lips together to make sure her lipstick was evenly applied.

Lela was just about to ask her what was her problem when a honey-dipped brother covered with a black Armani blazer and jeans approached them.

Trey yelled out, "Oh, this is my boy, Neil. Neil...Lela. Lela...Neil."

Lela recognized him as the guy who had been busy trying to flee a crowd of young ladies who seemed interested in their own private party. The ladies were practically drooling over him.

Lela was taken by surprise when Neil took her hand in his and kissed it, his lips lingering longer than an average friendly kiss.

Because their eyes were locked on each other, neither Lela nor Neil noticed Trey and Tonya staring at them. Without a doubt, Trey's friend had Lela's full attention.

Trey cleared his throat and added, "Neil works over at Naytek with me, cuz."

"I remember meeting you some years back, but nice to meet with you again, Neil," was Lela's reply to the teasing hand kiss. The last thing she wanted was to look like the desperate broads he just practically ran away from...and she definitely didn't need a rebound man. So, she shook the image playing in her head of this gentleman's lips touching her in more treasured places.

"Likewise," he said while massaging her hand which he still held.

"Okay." Lela moved her hand back to her side on the sly. She also moved her glance to Tonya to avert her attention from the intriguing man.

Tonya waited impatiently for Trey to acknowledge her standing there. To get attention, she cleared her throat. "And I am..."

"...her chicken head friend, Tonya," Trey joked. Trey had a thing for Tonya since seventh grade, but tried not to let it be known.

"I know you didn't go there. Whatever, Trey." Tonya shot Trey a look that only he knew what it meant, and then extended her hand to Neil for a handshake. Instead, he took her hand in his and placed a brief kiss on it.

The foursome became acquainted with each other while strolling to the club's entrance. At the door, as expected, Spanky started with his Mack Daddy mode. As he scanned down the front of her body with the metal detector, he eyeballed Lela like a kid would a lollipop.

Spanky smiled, showing off his platinum grill. "You know I've been missing me some Lela. Why you don't call a brotha sometimes?" When he walked around to scan her back with his wand, he added loudly, "Umph, umph, umph. It ought to be a law against it. I been missing this juicy booty of yours, too."

Silently wishing he would hurry up and do his job, Lela did well with ignoring him. That is, until he took it too far and rubbed her behind longer and more sensually than the job called for.

Lela spun around and tried to slap the taste out his mouth. "Keep your grimy hands off me Spanky! You can only wish you still had it like that."

About that time, Neil stepped up on sheer principle. "Back off my lady, man. It's not that type of party." Lela did walk up to the door at his side and, had she been his girl, what Spanky did was straight up disrespectful.

Lela turned around, surprised to see it was Trey's friend standing up for her honor.

Trey, on the other hand, was busy being courted by the same group of women Neil fled from earlier. When he caught wind of the commotion, he walked over to see what was going on.

"Go on in and get us a table, babe," Neil told Lela, while giving Spanky a look that said *"you don't want to see me like that"* as he walked by him and into the club. If it weren't for the realization that Spanky was armed with a glock, Neil would have rattled his jaw two minutes ago.

"Lela," Spanky sneered, "I know you not going to play me off for *this* punk nigga!"

Lela frowned like she had a sour taste in her mouth. "Who you calling a nigga? He has more going for himself than your still living at home with your momma butt ever will. If you don't chill out, you and your momma are going to be homeless. I'll make sure Tiny knows you're out here tripping, and you won't have your little job working this door. Have you forgotten who you're messing with Spanky? I can jump just as crazy as you are."

That said, Spanky dropped the matter and waved for the next couple to enter the club. "Go 'head on then," he said, like he could care one way or the other. "You wasn't all that anyway."

Inside, Lela found a table for four in the VIP section, which had plush maroon booths with candlelit, gold-plated tables. Once seated, Neil ordered a bottle of Courvoisier. Usually, Lela didn't drink when she went out, but after the day she had, she sipped on the glass of liquor like it was her lifeline.

After relaxing for a while, she announced to the group, "I'll be right back. I'm going to the ladies room."

Before she could gather her purse off the floor, Neil was on his feet. "Hold on. Let me get that for you." He pulled her chair out and helped her from her seat.

She unconsciously raised an eyebrow. *A keeper*? It wasn't until she came back to her seat to find him standing there, holding it out for her that she was sold on the idea.

All men treat you like a queen in the beginning, she reminded herself as she thought of Tyrese and their fantasy beginning.

She gathered from conversing with him that his name was Cornelius Johnston, but most of his friends called him Neil. He and Trey both worked for Naytek, a consulting firm, where Neil had been a sales manager for the last two years. Neil was recently promoted to vice president and that meant he would have to relocate to Atlanta. Naytek was almost the largest company in Opelika, second only to Auburn University. While it was obvious that he loved his job, the most important details were that he was single and he was 32 years old; Lela was definitely done with younger men, for good.

Neil was doing all the things a *man* was supposed to do without expecting her to bow down at his feet. One thing Lela hated about clubbing was when men thought buying a drink equaled butt-naked sex in some cheap hotel until four in the morning. She was quite capable of purchasing her own drink and may offer to purchase his under the right circumstances.

Lela could have sat there and talked to him all night just to inhale his seductive aroma. Unlike Tyrese who wore braids and white tees all the time, Neil had a baldhead and was dressed classy yet casual. As he moved closer to her, his baritone voice made her heart skip a beat…one beat away from Tyrese's drum.

"So, Lela," he said, "now that I've told you all about me, what about you? Tell me who I'm messing with." He hinted to what she told Spanky earlier.

"Well, first off, my name is Lela James. As far as men go, I've been through it all. As a matter of fact, I'm just getting out of a relationship where I was really feeling this guy. I mean, really. We were supposed to get married next year, but I caught him cheating today." She swallowed a lump in her throat. "I guess it's a good thing I found out what I was working with before I married him, huh?"

"Yes, it is. I know a little bit about that myself." His voice was sincere.

"And I have a six-year-old son who gets most of my time and attention, except for some weekends, like this one, when he's at my mother's house. Other than that, I'm like most grown folks, working and paying bills."

"You don't look old enough to have a six-year-old son," Neil said in amazement. He put her age at no more than 23. "What's his name?"

"Don't play!" she chuckled. "I'm 29, but thanks for the compliment. His name is Antwan."

"That's cool. What kind of work do you do?"

"Medical transcription. That involves typing up medical notes." Because very few people were aware of her profession, Lela was used to having to explain what her job entailed.

"I know what it is." Neil smiled. "It appears we have more in common than I thought. I'm a consultant in that field. I sell medical transcription services and software to hospitals throughout the nation for Naytek."

Lela finished off her second Long Island Iced Tea, and said, "so that is what you guys do over at Naytek. I never knew. Well, now I can put a face to one of the people making the big money in the transcription field."

"I wouldn't say all that," he replied, brushing off the truth.

"Don't be over here trying to take advantage of my cousin, man," Trey said as he and Tonya took a break from grinding on each other on the dance floor.

Neil flashed his million-dollar smile at Lela, ignoring Trey. "I'm just enjoying the lady's company, man, and I hope she's enjoying mines."

"Sure, I am." She attempted to sound somewhat disengaged, not wanting to allow herself to get caught up in his charm.

When the Cha-Cha song came on, Tonya practically dragged Lela by the arm toward the dance floor.

Lela pulled back. "I'm going to have to pass this time." She was too tight off Courvoisier and Long Island Teas to walk, much less dance. She had forgotten about all the wine she drank at home earlier in the evening, and Neil had kept the drinks coming one after the other. Now she was starting to regret accepting them.

When the beat to R. Kelly's "It Seems Like You're Ready" came on, it was Trey who pulled Tonya back out to the dance floor.

"I'm not feeling too hot," Lela confided in Neil once they were alone. "I think I need to head home. I'm going to go get Tonya so we can go. I'll be right ba..." Lela's head hit the table as she passed out. Her mini skirt had inched all the way up her thighs, and she was too drunk to even care.

Neil readjusted her clothing so her legs were not exposed, but not before admiring the full beauty of them.

When Trey and Tonya made it back to the table, they both asked, "What's wrong with Lela?" Trey eyed Neil suspiciously. He trusted Neil with his life, but gave him a hard time nonetheless.

"We were just sitting here talking and then she clunked out. She was putting the drinks down like she could handle them," Neil said, stress lines growing across his forehead.

Tonya shook Lela's shoulder in an attempt to wake her. "Girl, how many drinks did you have?" She looked around the table at the host of empty glasses and answered her own question.

"Let's go, Lela. You've had one too many." She shook her again. "You're going to have to walk though, 'cause I'm not carrying your heavy butt in the house."

Barely opening her eyes, Lela reached inside her purse and handed her house key to Neil. "Come on; let's go, baby."

Trey and Tonya looked at Lela like she was crazy. Neil looked flattered, but didn't take her up on the offer.

"I'll walk you to the car, Lela," Neil offered, placing the keys back inside her purse. "Tonya will make sure you get home safely."

Lela took his hand without protest. At Tonya's car, she took Neil by surprise by wrapping her small arms around his masculine neck and kissing him full on the lips.

Tonya had been so into her conversation with Trey that she didn't notice Lela trying to suck Neil's tongue out his throat. Once she did, she just stood there with her mouth open. When she got her faculties together, she shouted, "Oh my God! Trey, get your cousin and put her in the car."

"Come home with me tonight," Lela whispered softly.

"Let's get you home, Lela," Neil told her, defying his body he pulled away from her.

Trey opened the passenger door to the Chrysler 300. "Get in here, girl. Out here acting like a freak. And you," Trey turned to Neil, "I've told you to stop taking advantage of my drunk cousin."

Before Neil could explain, Lela blurted out, "Stay out of my business, Trey," and then passed out on the front seat.

"And who is supposed to help me get her out of the car? She can barely walk," Tonya questioned Trey.

"We'll follow you two to the house," Neil volunteered with pep in his voice.

Like the ride to the club, the ride home was quiet. This time because Lela slept the entire way. Pulling into the driveway, Neil got out of his car and offered to carry Lela. He placed her head securely on his chest and cradled her warm body close to his as he walked her into the house.

Standing in Lela's quaint bedroom, Neil could see himself in there spending *many* nights with her. He admired her beauty as she peacefully lay in her bed. He imagined himself sliding into her silky sheets and not coming out for months. *Not like this,* he reasoned with his aching body.

With lustful eyes, Neil asked Trey, "You think we should change her into some nightclothes?"

"I'll get her some when y'all leave," Tonya said as she pulled herself out of Trey's arms.

"Good try, man. The only way you are going to see Lela undressed is if she is awake and willing." Trey turned off the light and exited the room holding Tonya's hand, with Neil following close behind.

"I just wanted to make sure she was comfortable. You know, man, nothing more."

"Riiiight. Come on, man."

★ ★ ★

Neil woke up the next morning with Lela on his mind. When she kissed him in the parking lot, his first instinct was to push her away, but her lips were so sweet and soft he got lost in the kiss. There was a connection to her that he could not deny.

He was taken aback by the few intimate hours they shared. He usually didn't drink, but after walking in on Larna and her girlfriend in bed yesterday, he needed something to help him relax and just kick it. The night out at The Foxy Lady had done the trick.

Lela captured his attention without even trying. Usually, the thought of women in the club scene was for one-night stands, then business as usual by Monday morning.

This Monday morning, as he sat at his desk pressing to finish a project the advertising committee was working on, he had a different feeling he wasn't quite ready to follow up on. His wounds were still fresh from his soured relationship, so instead of chasing something new he focused on Naytek. He chalked Saturday night up to a good time and kept churning through the pile of work on his desk.

It probably was the alcohol working on both of us anyway, he told himself. His belief was if something was meant to be, it would become a reality in due time.

"Mr. Johnston, there is a Larna Darby on line one," the temp secretary buzzed Neil's personal line.

"Tell her I am in a meeting. As a matter of fact, whenever she calls, just take a message." Larna was the last person in the world he wanted to talk to.

He thought of Lela often after that night. Even after he transferred to Atlanta, he thought about her and what could have been, until often turned into ever so often, and ever so often turned into rarely.

<u>8</u>
Lady in Red

"Give me another, Paul, on the rocks," Neil told the bartender at Roasters in Atlanta. He was on his fifth shot of Hennessey and he lost count of how many beers he had drank.

"All right, buddy, but this is your last one," the burly bartender forewarned him. "I can't have you leaving out of here hurting yourself."

"I'm about to go home anyway. I just need one more for the road." Neil felt empty with only his career to fulfill him, and even his career left the glass half empty.

The bartender handed him the glass of brown fluid, which served as Neil's lifeline for the moment. He gulped half of it down with one swig.

"Thanks, man," Neil said, setting the glass down on a coaster. "Hey, let me ask you something."

"Sure. Go right ahead." The bartender gave a look to say he was used to people getting drunk and talking him to death.

"Have you ever had a woman taken from you by another woman?"

"I can't say I have, but that explains it."

"What?"

"That explains why you've been trying to drown your sorrows in liquor tonight. Man, you've got to be strong. What you should have done was asked to join the two ladies for a little hanky panky." The bartender adjusted the rubber band on his brunette ponytail and put on his leather rider jacket. He gave advice like a bar-side shrink.

"I couldn't with this one, man. It just...it just..."

"Hurt so bad? Is that what you're trying to say, fella?"

"Yeah." Neil looked around to make sure his conversation was not being eavesdropped on. He wasn't a punk about his, but he needed to talk about it to somebody. "It hurt, man. I loved that girl."

"I'm telling you if you go and screw both of 'em it will change that 'hurt so bad' to a 'hurt so good' feeling."

Neil laughed for the first time in twenty-four hours. "I guess you're right, man, but she's a wrap. I'm moving on."

"You and me both. Mind if I sit down?" A blonde with beautiful curls flowing down her back pointed to the seat beside his.

"Oh...no. By all means, go right ahead."

"I overheard part of your conversation, and like they say, misery loves company. So, I thought we would be good together. Maybe we could exchange war stories." She held her left hand out to him. He did not miss the fact that an expensive ring sheltered her ring finger. "Amanda...and you are?"

"Cornelius, but call me Neil."

"Well, nice to meet you, Neil." She beckoned the bartender, who looked to be preparing to close the bar. "An Appletini, please."

"Sure thing Miss."

"So like I was saying, we have a lot in common. Just be glad you were able to confront your wife."

"Girlfriend," Neil corrected.

"Well, be glad you were able to get some type of closure from your girlfriend. Nothing is worse than coming home to a Dear Jane letter after eight years of marriage."

"Eight years, and all dude left you with was a note? That's foul." *Almost as foul as finding your woman getting banged with a 14-inch dildo by her best friend.* Neil wouldn't dare share this tidbit with the two strangers.

"Yes...a frigging note," Amanda chimed through his horrid recollection of that night.

"All I can say is dude must have been blind to up and leave you like that." Neil figured there was more to the story.

"Yes, he was. I gave my life to him." Amanda dried a lone tear that threatened to run down her cheek. "But it's his loss."

"That's how I look at it, too." Neil gulped the last of his drink and asked the bartender for his tab.

"It was nice talking to you. Here's my card if you ever need someone to talk to. Like you said, misery loves company." He handed Amanda the tiny card and smiled.

"Why, thank you. I will be putting this to use."

When he walked off, she looked at the card. "Hey, wait a minute! You work for Naytek. You're *the* Cornelius Johnston, the vice president at Naytek?"

"That's me."

"I'm Amanda Broady. I start work there next Monday, and I hear you are going to be my boss."

"Really? So you're Christian's niece?"

"Yes."

"Well, I'll be seeing you," Neil said as he left the bar. He needed to get home ASAP before he passed out. He staggered to the curb and hailed a cab.

With Neil out of sight, she looked at the card once more. "Oh, you most definitely will be seeing me."

Part 2

Living Life Like It's Golden

9
A Greater Kind of Love

It had been six months since Lela and Tyrese broke up, and Lela was finally getting her life back on track. Tyrese had tried, to no avail, to get back with her, but she stood her ground. She had been hitting the gym and taking care of herself. Instead of putting her faith in a man, she put it in God. She had even started going to church and tithing more regularly. To this date, she had six months of celibacy under her belt. She couldn't believe she held out for six months, but she had.

Trey called her the morning after he and Neil dropped her off, teasing her about getting so drunk until she passed out. He also teased her about kissing Neil in the parking lot. After that night, she had not pursued Neil. Before opening another door, she wanted to make sure the door was nailed shut tight from her relationship with Tyrese. However, this did not stop Neil from invading her dreams nearly every night since that Saturday night six months earlier.

Tyrese had called and stopped by so many times that she had to get a restraining order and her phone numbers changed. Turns out, Sarah dumped him fast after her parents found out about them and threatened to disown her.

"Antwan, get the last bag by the door! We need to get going!" Lela yelled up the staircase to her son. She mimicked Cedric the Entertainer in the movie *Johnson's Family Vacation*, adding, "I-10 by 10."

They were on their way to the annual James Family Reunion in Atlanta, which was a two-hour drive from the small town of Opelika where she lived. She was not really looking forward to the drive or the reunion. Sometimes being around family, especially hers, was not all hugs, kisses, and old memories. They could get rowdy and be ready to fight in a heartbeat. Plus, there were the uppity members who never failed to have unwanted advice to share.

Then there were her aunts, who threw her a pity party every year because she was not married. They brought up everything they thought was wrong in Lela's life, which they believed kept her from finding a husband. If it wasn't for her mother, she would have told them a little something about what was wrong in their own lives a long time ago. Especially Aunt Jenny who still sported her 1970's afro with the green, black, and red African headband and matching clothes. Jenny couldn't have kids, but that didn't stop her husband from having three kids outside their marriage. Yeah, that's right...*three* outside kids by two different women. And to top it off, most weekends you could find Aunt Jenny walking through the mall with the three little kids trucking behind her whenever she babysat for her husband. Lela's main question was *who needs to pity who?*

"I'm coming, Momma," Antwan responded, breaking her thoughts. He still had his PlayStation game controller in his hand playing Mortal Combat.

"Do I still hear that game?" She knew she heard it. "Don't make me have to come up there and get you, Antwan Jamar Miller."

Hearing his full name, Antwan turned off the game, picked up his Game Boy pouch, and went downstairs. He pushed his rolling Spiderman luggage bag to the trunk, and Lela placed it inside.

"I can't wait to get in the pool. I can get in the deep end this year since I've been taking my lessons."

"No. We're going to stick with the three feet, and if you keep ignoring me like you just did, you won't be getting in the pool at all." She raised her balled fist and shook it in front of each eye, gesturing of a spanking.

"Buckle up. We've got a long ride ahead of us."

Antwan getting in the pool was not something Lela was looking forward to. He had nearly drowned at the local water park when he was only four. Even though that was two years ago, she was still pained when she thought of the day she made a near fatal mistake.

At the water park that day, Antwan had been begging her to get into the wave pool. Lela was not a swimmer, but she promised him that they could get in the shallow end. "Let me get us a float, Antwan, and then we will get in," she said as she walked to the booth to purchase a float with him at her side.

"Yes, ma'am."

The line was long because it was a holiday, and Lela allowed her mind to drift, thinking about errands she had to run after they left the park. She had a bad habit of going off into her own world, and while standing in the line, she was definitely in her own zone. She must have been standing in line for five minutes when she heard the commotion of people running toward the wave pool. Then a bodyguard carrying a lifeless, ashen-looking toddler ran to the poolside.

Her first instinct was to reach for Antwan's hand, but he wasn't beside her anymore. She panicked, frantically searching the area for him and calling his name. When he didn't turn up, she pushed people out of the way, trying to make it through the crowd to see the identity of the child whom the bodyguard pulled from the pool.

"Oh my God! It's my baby!" Even after seeing that the child was wearing the same swimming trunks as Antwan had on, she didn't want to believe it was him. He had just been at her side babbling about how much he wanted to get in the wave pool. She stood in shock and then screamed as a river of tears fell from her eyes. "Antwan!" she screamed at the top of her lungs.

The only thing she remembered was someone saying, "That's the mother. Someone console the mother."

Lela begged God for mercy. "God...please spare my son! God, please take me instead. Don't take my baby. Lord, please give him a chance to live. Forgive me for my sins. Don't make me pay for them with my son. God... " As she prayed, repented, and asked for mercy, she could feel the holy spirit envelop her.

The lifeguards were able to revive him, and since he was not underwater long he was lucky enough not to have suffered any brain damage or medical complications from loss of oxygen.

Lela thought he would be scared of pools after that, but every chance he got he was swimming. The thought of him being in deep water made Lela nervous to no end. Still, she knew she had to look past her fears and allow him to do what he loved. She was glad she put him in swimming lessons this year. Now, he was swimming like a fish.

Whenever she would give testimony about the grace of God, that day served as her story.

She put her arm on his shoulder, kissed his cheek, and sent up a silent "thank you" to God for giving her precious son to her, not only once, but twice.

She backed out of her driveway and cruised through the neighborhood, which was lined with modest homes. The houses were just big enough for a small family, and most were occupied by blue-collar workers. Lela and Antwan's home was a three-bedroom brick house. Though the houses were far from the five-hundred-thousand plus dollar vintage homes on the ritzy side of town, she was proud to have a place of her own.

She worked from home, and while hers was not a money-spinning career, she made enough to maintain their cozy lifestyle. It also helped that she managed her money well. Frugality permitted her to keep her mortgage and bills paid, clothe her son, and put food on the table. And for the past six months with no man to interfere, she had been able to see the fruits of her labor. She finally started to build her savings and retirement account. *Four thousand dollars saved since I got rid of Tyrese.*

After gassing up, she hit the highway to Atlanta on I-85 North.

The family reunion was being hosted at the Hilton Garden Inn in Atlanta, so her savings account would take a slight hit. Antwan always had a ball at the reunions, and this was the only vacation they took every year, so it was worth it. She caught a glimpse of her son in the rearview mirror playing his portable Game Boy Advance, and wished she had grabbed her Mul-Ty CD from her dresser to help pass the time. After primping her silky curly weave that she got retouched yesterday, she fumbled with the radio until she found Hot 105.7, and then set the Jeep on cruise control.

10

We are Family

Check-in time was two o'clock, so Lela and Antwan had lunch in the Hilton Café. Once checked in, she and Antwan dressed for the picnic and drove to Keisel Park. Before she could get out of the car good, she heard Uncle Calvin's voice blasting through the speakers.

"The James are back together once again! Watch out now, Grandma!" Calvin shouted.

"There's nothing like family, babe," Lela told Antwan while shaking her head. "Remember that."

Excited to see his young male cousins, Antwan scurried toward the crowd, bypassing all the girls who he said had the cooties.

Lela saw Calvin mouth to his wife, Dawn, of twenty-eight years to bring him something to drink. Dawn winked at him and sashayed over to the bar like a teenage girl in love. He watched her every move, nodding his head and licking his lips.

"Mercy! Let's bump a little Nelly. It's getting hot in herrrrr," Calvin said as he winked back at Dawn and adjusted his pants on the sly.

Lela watched the playful exchange between her aunt and uncle, and wondered if she would be so lucky to find a husband who would still be putty in her hands after twenty-eight years of marriage. Seeing her uncle and aunt together always made her wish she could find in a mate a fraction of the affection they shared for each other.

Dawn was one aunt that Lela did like. It figures she got along with her uncle's wife but not any of her blood aunts. Speaking of the evil trio, they all seemed to spot Lela at the same time. Jenny, Lacy, and Tab were all sitting under a shade tree and waved Lela over. Being cordial, she went over and hugged each of them before making an excuse to keep it moving.

"Hey, Lela baby, when are you going to bring a man with you?" Aunt Lacy asked, starting the line of questioning.

"Where is that fine thing you had with you last year?" Aunt Tab chimed in.

"What you need to do is get yourself a husband like my Robert," Aunt Jenny preached.

Lela was just about to let Aunt Jenny know what she could do with her two-baby-momma-having husband when she saw Grandma Jana. Quickly, she walked over to her grandmother's table.

"Grandma! How are you?" This was the main person Lela could not wait to lay her eyes on. She had not seen her grandma since she flew out to see her over a year ago.

"I'm fine, baby. Where's that big boy of yours? He hasn't even came and kissed his great-grandma yet."

"He hasn't? You know how these boys are. Once they get together, that's it. I'll make sure to send him your way when I find him." Lela chuckled. Grandma Jana always put her in the highest spirits.

"Well, how you been, sweet pea?"

"Just fine, Grandma. How about you? Have you been back to see the heart doctor?"

"Yes. He told me everything will be fine as long as I eat right and exercise."

Grandma Jana was seventy five, but she would put a young girl to shame during a workout. "Enough about me. When are you gonna get married, child. A beautiful girl like yourself should have no problem finding a man."

"Not you, too, Grandma. I just ran away from Jenny, Lacy, and Tab, who were nagging me about the same thing. If you must know, it's not finding a man that's the problem. I've found plenty. It's finding one that will do right by me *and* Antwan."

Grandma Jana leaned in close and spoke in a whisper. "You want your grandma to show you how it's done?"

Lela wondered where her grandma was taking this. With Grandma Jana, it could be anywhere.

"How what's done?"

"Picking up a man and making him do right."

Hesitantly, Lela answered, "Okay then. Show me what you working with, Grandma."

Within seconds, Grandma Jana pranced off in the direction of an older gentleman who was hiking up toward the parking area with his fishing gear. Grandma Jana had her hand on her hip, and Lela didn't want to think about what her grandmother was going to say to the unsuspecting man.

When the man reached into his vehicle and pulled out a small card, handing it to Grandma Jana, Lela stood in disbelief. *Go on and work it then, Grandma.* Between Grandma Jana and Tonya she had two divas as best friends.

If any of Lela's other family knew Grandma Jana was over there picking up a man, they would have tried to stop her. But they were none the wiser, as they were all gathered under the canopy that was draped with a "Welcome to the James Family Reunion 2005" banner.

Music boomed from the speakers. As usual, Uncle Calvin was doubling as DJ and cook. He sported a Michael Jordan jersey, some baggy FUBU jeans, and a pair of Air Jordan sneakers on his feet. Even though he was knocking on fifty's door, he still dressed more hip than most teenagers.

Everyone was having a ball laughing and reminiscing about old times. Until, like clockwork, the story came up about Lela's uncles fighting in the middle of the road in their teens. That's when Calvin and John started fussing all over again about who won the fight.

Someone brought the fight up every year and they would have the same argument, every year. Grandma Jana had four girls and two boys. The girls got along good, but her boys had a pure sibling rivalry thing going on.

"No, no, man," Uncle John argued. "I tore you up and you know it. The only reason I let you up was because people were talking about calling the police."

Then Calvin said, "Yeah and that's when I grabbed you by the balls and tried to yank 'em off. Remember they had to take you to the emergency room and everythang, man. Don't be trying to act brand new in front of your wife and kids, man. Just go on and say it, I whipped you and that's it." He recounted the fight with pride.

Various family members laughed at the thought of Uncle John doubled over with Uncle Calvin squeezing the life out of his manhood.

Lela's mother, Rachel, who had been snapping pictures of

Antwan, came to the canopy to diffuse the fight. "Y'all stop the foolishness. I won the fight. Momma sent me out there with a belt to whip the both of you." Rachel spoke with the authority of an oldest child. "Now if y'all don't want me to tell some stories about how I used to whip both of your butts...like the time Calvin tried to sneak Bessie Ann through the window when he was thirteen..."

Calvin coughed like he was choking. "Um...no need to get into all that. I got to go check on this meat anyway."

"That's what I thought," Rachel said.

* * *

Later that afternoon, Lela sat poolside watching Antwan and some of his little cousins swim in the hotel's pool. Kids were all over the place. Antwan showed off his skills from the swimming lessons as he glided through the three feet of water like a pro. He had been looking forward to the family reunion so he could see his cousins again and show off in the pool, and his cousins were just as excited to see his new moves.

After laying down the ground rules about pool safety, Lela sat back on her lounge chair half reading a novel. Most of her attention was on the kids in the pool. She removed her beach towel that was wrapped around her waist, exposing her yellow bikini. No sooner than she removed it, she sensed Punkin was heading into deeper water than she could handle.

"Come back this way, Punkin!" Lela said to her little cousin. "You are getting too close to the deep end."

Before she could jump in after Punkin, a handsome gentleman touched her on the shoulder and said, "Let me get her for you." His voice was so masculine, it bordered on seductive. His simple touch on the shoulder sent twinges through her spine. She was taken aback by his physique that was so on point, she almost forgot about Punkin. A warm breeze of air brought her back to reality.

Punkin was on her tippy toes trying to make it back to shallow water and he reached her within seconds. He brought the pony-tailed little girl back past the three feet marker.

Lela decided to get in the pool to be near the kids just in case one of them tried to pull a fast one again. The gentleman stayed in the pool, too.

It had been six months since they last laid eyes on each other, but the dark lighting in the club mixed with alcohol did no justice to the sight she was seeing before her. Neil was one handsome man. Every chance she got, she admired his fit body stroking through the cool water in the pool.

They eyed each other, but neither spoke more than two words to the other.

Lela could not believe how tense she was around him. She normally exuded self confidence when around men, but the countless failed relationships left her feeling inadequate or incapable of interacting with potentially good men.

Even though she tried to get in her confident zone again, she couldn't get up enough nerve to approach Neil. Without the Courvoisier in her system, like that night at the club, she could see herself getting nowhere with him unless he took the lead.

Every chance Lela got she would sneak a peek at Neil's broad shoulders and masculine chest. His six pack down to the bulge in his swim trunks took her to a whole new level of horniness. *Hey, it had been six months.* She noticed him looking at her breasts, and the fact that he was checking her out made him look even hotter. She had to get out of the pool and fast. Being in the same vicinity as him was driving her crazy. After getting out, she asked Aunt Dawn, who was poolside, to watch the kids for a minute while she fetched something from her room.

"Uh…we've been out here a while, so I need to get more suntan lotion for myself and the kids," she lied, excusing herself. On her way to the room, she took a deep breath and tried to shake this man from her thoughts, though beautiful thoughts indeed.

Neil couldn't get over the beautiful enchantress that he stole a glimpse of every chance he could get. Just the thought of her sharing the same space with him in the pool raised the water temperature ten degrees. He attempted to avoid gazing at her voluptuous breasts, but temptation got the best of him. When she emerged from the pool, her bikini damn near drove him wild. Her curvaceous body in that bikini had him rehearsing his wedding vows.

I take this woman… His body threatened to respond, and he had to desperately talk himself out of it. A pool full of kids was definitely not the place to have those type of feelings, but *mercy, this lady!*

The way her hips swayed as she walked he could barely keep himself calm. If he did not think fast, soon his inevitable arousal would make a public appearance. He was glad when she walked out of sight so he could will his body back under control.

11
Shaken

The elevator arrived on the eighth floor. Just as Lela stepped off, she bumped into her cousin Trey.

Trey had been late getting there, so this was their first time seeing each other. Before their unexpected meeting at the club six months earlier, it had been over a year since they had last seen each other, despite living in the same town.

They were excited to see one another again. While growing up, they were always referred to as Bonnie and Clyde. Always in trouble. Lela's mother, Rachel, and Trey's father, Calvin, were very close and even lived together for a few years. Hence, Lela and Trey grew up very close.

"Hey, Trey." Lela's smile was wide and radiant.

"Hey, Lela. Come here." He extended his arms and gave his little cousin a bear hug.

She returned his hug tightly around the neck. They engaged in some small talk for a few minutes, until she took the opportunity to ask about the object of her attention. She pointed out of the glass window toward the pool.

"So I see your friend is with you?" she said as she fought putting her hands over her face. What she could remember from the night they met was not something she was proud of.

When Trey flashed his flawless grin, Lela could see why he drove so many women crazy. He was handsome, cousin or not. Standing 6 feet 4 inches, he had a sturdy frame with a smile so warm it could melt butter.

"Oh yeah, my boy Neil. His sister is getting married in August, and he didn't want to have to make the trip twice since his family is in Denver. I wouldn't hear of my boy staying at home by himself, so I invited him to spend the holiday with us."

Neil jumped on the offer, too, expecting to see Lela again. Trey observed Lela's reaction to his answer and tilted his head, already knowing the answer to his next question.

"Why you asking about him? You interested?"

"Just wondering." Then she fished for more info. "Home *alone*. That must mean no girlfriend?"

"No, he's single, and between me and you, the man has asked about you more than a couple times since The Foxy Lady."

"I see." Lela shifted the subject, not wanting to sound too obviously interested. "How you liking your new job, big timer? You all up in the big leagues now. Moving on up," she sang, imitating the Jefferson's theme song. "Everyone has been bragging about you. Grandma has been telling everyone about your *Escalator*," she added, laughing. Their grandmother was always making up names for *"things ya'll kids have nowadays."*

He shook his head and laughed at their grandmother's pronunciation. "I took Grandma for a ride this morning. And you, you'll have to come over to my place some time and see how I'm living for yourself. I just live what ten, fifteen minutes away from you?" He raised his eyebrow and returned to the more interesting topic.

"Don't try to change the subject, Lela. Do you want me to hook you up with my boy?" He waited for her to respond, and when she didn't, he said, "He's good people. I told you he's single. You know I wouldn't even hook you up if he was up to no good."

Then, out of nowhere, as if he had a flashback of some of the guys Lela had brought home before, he said, "He's not like the dudes you're used to kicking it with. He's drama free. And he's not thug material. Dude is all about the business. Are you able to roll with a straight-up brother like that?" With two shakes of the head, he added, "No drama. No, no drama. I'm not saying you got that. I'm just saying my boy ain't gonna deal with that."

Lela put her hand up and rolled her eyes. Instantly, her attitude changed from sugar to tart. "Honey boom! If he's a man about his, then he can handle a little drama in his life. Plus, I'm not into thugs, and definitely not drama, anymore. Too many problems."

A slight stab of grief set deep in her eyes. In a flash, she remembered her prior sorry excuses for relationships, including her latest with Tyrese. She had definitely had her fair share of ruffians. *No more good for nothing jokers for me,* she thought.

Then, in a more solemn tone, she continued, "For real, I'm looking for a good man, even if it's not Neil. I'm tired of giving all of me and getting only a quarter percent back. You feel me? I've had to put all old dogs on foot patrol. Tired of the games. So yes, my next man will be free of drama, or I will have no man at all. I haven't done too bad by myself the past six months."

"Is that right?" he asked, finding it hard to believe she was not still living it up ghetto fabulous with one of her old flames. "You know you love you some Big Nate, Pookie, Smokey type brothers. I can't see you living the square life."

"I see you still got jokes, but you heard me right. I'm like Mary J. No more drama." She snapped her fingers and sung in tune to Mary J's beat. "Besides, I've been a lot of things: opinionated, strong willed, and outgoing. But ghetto fab? Come on. Give your girl a little more credit than that."

Trey smiled, glad to hear his cousin had finally come to her senses in the man department. He'd admired Lela's sweet personality and her drive for success long before she knew she had it. "I always knew you had more class than you let on. This is good to hear because I'm getting too old to be fighting for your butt."

They both laughed.

"Oh, like I haven't had to stomp a few girls back in the day for slashing your tires, or what about the time Keisha tried to fight Aunt Dawn and I had to regulate on her?"

They laughed some more.

Those were a few instances Trey had been successful in forgetting. Funny he had not forgotten Lela's indiscretions, but had long since forgotten his own.

Remembering that she needed to get back to the pool to relieve Aunt Dawn, Lela said, "Look, Trey, I'll catch up with you later. I'm headed to my room for some suntan lotion. Tell your boy to come put it on for me." Once she heard it with her own ears, she couldn't believe she said it, and she knew Trey would be repeating it. "I'm just kidding," she added quickly. "Just kidding."

"You ain't kidding. I'ma tell him. I'm sure he'd be down with it."

"I was *just* playing." But was she really? Being turned on wasn't an outfit she wore discreetly. Sharing the same space with Neil in the pool had her yearning for him to apply the lotion for her.

Trey turned and pressed the down button on the elevator. "All right then. I'm about to dip off in this pool for a little bit. Later, cuz."

"Later." She walked to her room with a smile. Trey's friend was single and a great catch, so her day was getting better by the moment.

Holding the elevator open, Trey asked, "Le, why didn't you invite Tonya?"

"What? You wanted me to?" Seemed like Lela was not the only one crushing.

"Never mind," Trey said while pressing the button to close the elevator doors.

What Lela didn't know was that Neil had already gotten the 411 on her from Trey, too. He had been checking her out since he first laid eyes on her today. Trey didn't tell her that little bit of info, though. He wanted to let Neil approach her without it looking like he was playing love connection for the two.

Lela took a few moments in her hotel room to get her mind right. The past six months she had thrown herself into her work and decided that her life goal would include getting closer to God, being a better parent to her son and planning for their future financially. After her last few relationships, she had come to realize that men were not worth the headache or heartache. The next time she fell in love, she would really have to fall. It would have to sneak up on her, and knock her off her feet. Kind of like what Neil's sheer presence was doing to her.

Approaching thirty years old had its bearings on her wanting to do things that would enhance her life, like increasing her personal wealth and raising her son right so he could grow into a responsible man. At the rate she was going with men, there was no way she was setting a good example for Antwan. She had always wanted to complete her family with a husband, who would be a stepfather to Antwan, but that was not top priority anymore. Therefore, while physically she was strongly attracted to Neil, she decided to look past the physical to more lasting qualities. Being single with her priorities in order, there was a continuous struggle to stay focused.

"Neil, you remember my cousin Lela." Lela was back at the

poolside, and Trey reintroduced her to Neil.

"Yeah," Neil replied.

Lela knew Trey was setting her up.

"Well good. You two chit-chat while I go check out the red skirt that just walked in. Ummmm, I don't think she's family." Trey rubbed his palms together as he walked over to the girl.

Lela stared nervously at Neil, wondering who would speak first.

Breaking the ice, he said, "So, Lela, it's nice to finally get the attention of the lady who has had my eye all day. I hoped that I didn't run you off from the pool earlier."

This was the first time she had an up-close look at his face, and it was gorgeous. His prominent cheekbone and luscious lips had her in a daze for what seemed like hours. The dim club lighting had done him no justice.

She snapped out of her trance and looked dreamily into his eyes as she spoke. "I have to admit I've been checking you out, too." She could feel his eyes piercing her skin as he checked out every curve on her body. She tried to focus, but her vision was getting more blurry by the second.

"Are you coming to the family banquet tonight?" she asked.

"If you will be there, most definitely." He took her hand in his and gave her that lingering kiss like he did that night at the club.

"Okay...I'll see you then." She moved her hand and made a dash over to the pool to retrieve Antwan so they could go get ready for the banquet. She could think of several things to do with Neil tonight rather than share space with him at the buffet. Desperately, she tried to shake him from her mind, because she felt too many emotions for someone she knew so little about...and that scared her.

12
Sweet Lady

The family gathered in the hotel's beautiful beige and cream decorated banquet hall. From the tablecloths to the flower arrangements, everything was immaculate. Lela was taken aback by how beautiful everything was and commended her mother and aunts for putting everything together so superbly. Aaliyah's "At Your Best" playing softly in the background set a festive and amorous mood.

Before Lela could get comfortable in her seat, she noticed her mother motioning for her to come join her in the kitchen. It was like a sixth sense her mother had. She could always tell when her daughter was near. "Come here, baby girl," Miss Rachel mouthed.

Lela never volunteered to work at the family reunion, yet her mom always made sure she put her to work. That is why Lela avoided the kitchen when she entered the banquet hall and went straight to the table reserved for her and Antwan.

Shoot, Lela thought. She was going to escape the sweatshop tonight, and was about to let her mother know.

As she headed to the kitchen, she thought of several different reasons she could tell her mother as to why she was not going to serve dinner tonight. One, she paid her money to enjoy herself. And two, she paid her money to enjoy herself. Halfway to the kitchen, she felt a warm touch and looked down to see a large, masculine hand covering hers.

"Do you think you're going to get to ignore me tonight?" He smiled, exposing a right-sided dimple she had not noticed earlier.

Her words momentarily stuck in her throat. She took a couple moments to drink in the essence of the man standing in front of her. His muscular arms in his Giovanni jacket were beckoning for her to rest in them.

"Of course not. I just got here. I was going to come to your table as soon as I see what it is my mother wants."

Lela noticed Rachel now had both hands on her hips looking in her direction.

"And it looks like my mother is about to put me to work in the kitchen, so I may not see much of anything but macaroni and cheese and string beans tonight," Lela pouted.

Neil smiled as he gave her one of his trademark hand strokes while his eyes surveyed her clingy gold sundress. "I will make sure we get some time together before tonight is over. You can bet on that." He pulled her to him in a brief hug, but long enough for his scent to linger on her skin. And long enough for her to feel the passion burning between them. "So save some energy for me. You're going to need it." His voice suggested much more than a dance.

"Yes, sir." Lela slowly backed away from him, almost bumping into a banister. She would serve a thousand pieces of chicken if it meant he was her payment for it.

"Took you long enough," her mother said after Lela joined her in the kitchen. "Help me take these pans out to the buffet table. And then put ice in those there cups and pour these drinks in them." Miss Rachel, as usual, skipped the pleasantries and put Lela straight to work. She was spouting out orders so quickly, Lela could barely keep up.

Noting that her mother had not said so much as 'hello,' Lela responded, "I'm fine, and you?"

"Don't get sassy." Miss Rachel stuck her cheek out for a kiss. Something she always did.

Lela kissed her mother lightly on the cheek, not wanting to mess up Miss Rachel's makeup any more than it already was. Her mother was all made up and looking like Patti Labelle's twin sister. But, instead of enjoying herself inside her beautiful skin, she wanted to sweat it out serving.

If Lela had it her way, she would set the food out and let everyone fix their own plates, buffet style. She helped Rachel unload the serving dishes onto the buffet table, but let her mother know she would only be helping for a few minutes.

One hour later, Lela was wiping sweat from her head as she

scooped food onto the plates. "Would you like some mashed potatoes?"

There were two lines going, but Neil made it a point to wait in Lela's line even though it was longer. A few of Lela's aunts waved him over to come through the shorter line, but he insisted on waiting in Lela's.

"Mashed pota…"

"I'll get that." Neil took the serving utensil from her hand. "Don't get me wrong, if I were in the mood to be served, I wouldn't have anyone serve me but you tonight. But, babe, you look tired. You should take a break. Come eat with me."

Lela noticed he had two plates in his hand.

"Plus, you owe me a dance," Neil reminded her.

Lela was flushed from standing on her feet, but the man in front of her was working on all of her senses in a way they had never been worked on before. She took a few more seconds to take in all he was saying to her.

Lela wiped the sweat off her forehead with a napkin and licked her lips instinctively. Subconsciously, she wanted to press her lips to his and tell him "Hell yes, you can have that dance right now. What would you like, a table or a lap dance?"

Instead, she snapped back to reality and giddily replied, "Sure." She looked in her mother's direction and added, "That's if my *momma* lets me off work."

"Honey child, the crowd done just about died down. Go on and mingle with the young folks," her mother grinned.

"Give me a minute and I'll meet you at your table," Lela told Neil as she removed her apron and excused herself to the restroom to freshen up.

In the restroom, Lela used her emergency beauty kit to primp her hair and reapply her makeup. It was a task getting the smell of collard greens and chicken out of her clothes, but she managed to do so. When she arrived back to the banquet hall, Neil had a table for four in the corner, where he had been sitting with Antwan and Trey before Trey took to the dance floor. The three of them small talked, and Neil ate while Lela picked over her food, all of her attention on him.

With everybody having gotten their eat on, the party started to get crunk. People were on the dance floor leaning with it, shaking their laffy taffies, or walking it out. The elders were keeping it simple with the two step, and couldn't nobody tell them they weren't getting down. Grandma Jana led the pack.

"The butterfly, uh..uh, that's old. Let me see you tootsie roll. Oh, get it, get it. To the left, to the right, to the front, to the back. Now slide, slide. Come on now, slide. Dip, baby, dip! " Calvin emulated the 69 Boys' "Tootsie Roll" track as it blasted through the speakers.

"Go, Big Momma Pearl. Go'on, Momma Jana. That's my momma, y'all. She still got it." Lela's grandmas and great grandmas were breaking it down so hard, Lela couldn't help but laugh.

Antwan and his cousins had their own little circle going, and they were all jumping around, doing backward flips, and dancing their little hearts out.

By this time, Aunt Tab had pulled Neil out on the floor and was doing her booty dance. His eyes stayed fixed on Lela the whole time, as if he was beckoning for her to rescue him. Lela laughed her butt off at the surprised look on Neil's face when her aunt dropped it like it was hot and started gyrating on him. The look on his face was priceless. Aunt Tab could cut up on the dance floor, and Neil was about to find out just how much.

"Ain't that right, man?" Trey said, breaking Lela from her thoughts.

Lela looked at Trey with a blank expression. "What was that?"

Trey began to repeat his statement, when Neil walked over and took her hand.

Her heart nearly pounced out of her skin watching him approach the table. Her body was pulsating so hard, she was afraid someone would hear it. She knew she had to be blushing, and hoped she didn't look googly eyed. Despite her obvious desire for this man, she attempted in vain to put her diva face on.

"You didn't think I would forget about that dance, did you? Come here." He intertwined her hand with his and led her to the dance floor.

Speechless, Lela neither declined nor accepted, though she could not have fixed her lips to say no if she wanted to.

"Well, I'll talk to you about that later then, Lela," Trey said, observing the lovebirds.

"Yeah, okay," Lela answered, not bothering to even look in Trey's direction.

"You could have saved me from your aunt, you know?"

"Why? Aunt Tab is harmless. Plus, you looked like you were enjoying the moves she was putting on you."

"Let's just see if those *moves* run in the family," Neil challenged her.

After their first dance to a fast beat, Miss Rachel tapped Lela on her shoulder and whispered in her ear that she was heading to her room.

"Antwan looks sleepy, and I'm fit to be tired, so I'm going to take him on up to my room with me. You can come get him in the morning." If Lela didn't know better, she could have sworn her mother gave her a *knowing* look, winked at her, and then said, "Have fun, baby."

"Okay. Thanks, Ma." Her words were music to Lela's ears. *Antwan's spending the night in my mom's room. Now, what can I do with this hunk of chocolate in front of me? I wonder if he knows what kind of fire he is setting.*

She took her place back in his arms, and they danced to every song until the music stopped. The old adage was true for them. They danced right into each other's hearts. The song of the evening was "Sweet Lady" by Tyrese.

"Sweet lady, would you be my sweet love for a lifetime. I'll be there when you need me. Just call and receive me." Neil whispered the chorus into her ear. He was not a singer, but his words fell on her ears better than the singer's ever could.

She was already on fire, but his hot breath on her earlobe and the pleasant sound of his voice had her boiling hot. She laid her head on his chest and allowed his scent to penetrate her nostrils and take her to new heights.

They held onto each other long after the song ended.

"This feels so right," Lela said, not wanting to let him go.

"I'll walk you and Antwan up to your room."

"My mother took him up already. He's staying with her in her suite tonight. But I'd like for you to walk *me* to my room."

$$\star\,\star\,\star$$

Neil's mind went full speed thinking of all the things he'd like to do to her. He would first plant kisses all over her body. Then scoop her into his arms, lay her gently on the bed, and have his way with her. He could feel her naked skin in his thoughts. He felt as if no one else was in the room but him and her. *She must be the one,* he thought. The thought of the 'L' word dancing through his mind made him nervous. The memory of the only other person he had ever told the "L" word to threatened to ruin his mood.

Hearing her ask him to walk her to her room brought new life to his manhood. He attempted in vain to will it down by thinking about something else. It was too soon.

They strolled down the hall, hand in hand, talking. Even on the elevator, they laughed and talked like old friends…and new lovers.

Once they reached her room, she decided to end the night quick before doing something she would regret in the morning.

"I had a nice…" Before she could get the words out, his lips covered hers with an intense kiss like none she'd ever experienced before, causing several murmurs to flow from her lips as he gently moved his tongue in and out of her mouth. She grabbed the back of his neck and pressed her body as close to his as she could manage.

He rubbed up and down her back, allowing his hand to explore every inch of her bodacious backside. If he never had a chance to touch her again, he would have had his fill tonight.

"Um, you'd better go. I'll see you tomorrow, right?" Lela said, hoping he would ignore her, pick her up, carry her over the threshold into her room, and blow her back out.

Neil invaded her fantasy. "Of course, you will. You won't be getting rid of me that easy. I'll call you when I get home…and tomorrow…and the next day."

"We'll see," Lela replied, as if she had heard that line before.

Neil's cell phone vibrated in his pocket. He had been ignoring it all night, but decided to answer this time in case it was an emergency. "Hold that thought. Let me answer her call."

Her call, Lela took a step back. *Oh no. I don't have time for the bullshit. I am not putting myself out there like that again.* She was glad to be getting this wake-up call sooner than later.

"Hello, Amanda. Is there a problem?" He kept his eyes on Lela as he answered what seemed like a thousand questions.

"I'm at Trey's family reunion. No. I think we are good to go on that one. Yes. Well, I'll be home tomorrow night. Yeah, I'm staying the weekend. It's at the Hilton. Ahh, yes. I forgot about that. Come over tomorrow evening around six and we will discuss it then. Get you some rest. It's Saturday night and you shouldn't be worrying about work, especially at two in the morning. Yeah, that one is not due for two more weeks. Don't work yourself to death. Alright, good night."

He flipped his cell phone closed. "Now…where were we?"

"Just about to say good night." Lela's soft voice was now dripping with attitude.

"I know we are just getting to know each other, but I'm going to be real with you. I'm falling for you. If it's any consolation, that was my CEO's niece. I am showing her the ropes around Naytek. She's kind of a workaholic, so she is always calling me at random times of the day *and night* with work-related questions."

"You don't owe me an explanation."

"I know, but it felt appropriate." He pulled her into another kiss. "Good night, Lela."

She gently pulled away and used her cardkey to enter her room. Once inside, she leaned her back up against the door and said, "Good night." She fell onto the bed and sent up a quick prayer.

Lord, please don't let me fall in love with another playa. I can't take any more heartache. Guide me with this one Lord, please.

13
Crazed Love

A manda sat in her candle-lit bedroom holding the phone to her bosom. Hearing Neil's voice made her feel good. When he finally answered his phone at two in the morning, she was relieved she didn't hear a woman's voice in the background. If he was dating someone, he would have told her. She could not understand why he would make plans for the weekend and not make her aware of them when they last talked Friday, so she was glad to hear he was just hanging out with Trey.

She had been crushing on Neil on the low ever since her uncle first introduced him as her trainer, but lately, she had been really playing him close, always calling him, and forgetting to tell him things in the office so she would have an excuse to call or come by his house.

Amanda had never been with a black man before. She was mad attracted to black men, but never had the nerve to do the "jungle fever" love thing for fear of what her family would think. She knew from dinner table talk that her father, uncles, and especially her grandfather, would disown her if she brought Neil home, but she didn't care in the least. He was a successful, intelligent, attentive and handsome hunk of a specimen, and he was going to be hers if it was the last thing she did.

She put the phone on the hook and picked up Naytek's September newsletter from her nightstand. A large picture of Neil with his arm around Amanda's shoulders, and her smiling from cheek to cheek, covered the front page. She and Neil had closed their first major transcription service deal together that day.

The more she looked at their picture together, the deeper her desire for him burned. They were meant for each other, equally yoked as far as she could see. She smiled as she pictured their future together, two boardroom powerhouses by day, and a loving family by night. She could see two or three beautiful children running through their lavish home. Their life would be perfect.

She allowed her soothing hand to gently inch down her smooth vanilla stomach toward the aching between her legs. She imagined it was Neil's hand as she stroked herself harder and harder. As soon as she released, she placed the picture back on her nightstand.

"Goodnight, Neil. One day, we'll be together." She stared into Neil's eyes in the photo on her nightstand until her eyes got too weak to stay open.

14
Too Addictive

Neil could not get Lela off of his mind. After leaving her room, he went back to the room he shared with Trey. All he and Lela had done was talk, dance, and share a kiss, yet he wanted her to be lying in his bed next to him more than anything. When he laid eyes on her at the pool, he decided to take Trey up on his offer to spend the entire weekend at the family reunion.

Trey told Neil at the banquet that he wouldn't be staying in the room they shared that night. He had hooked up with the girl he was talking to at the pool earlier that day.

At least my boy is getting some action, Neil hinted as he laid his semi hard body down on the bed. He remembered to call Lela and give her their room number, which was only five doors down from her suite.

"Thanks for making my night. You are a very special woman, Lela James. I look forward to getting to know a lot more about you."

"Back at you, babe. Goodnight, Neil."

"Goodnight."

Hanging up the phone, Lela let her mind drift to Neil's sophisticated demeanor as he met and greeted her family throughout the day and night. She thought back to his stamina as he played volleyball with her cousins earlier that day. Seeing his muscles flex as he walked, jumped, and swam was about all she could take. Not to mention the way he seduced her on the ballroom floor and his kiss that lingered on her lips. She tossed and turned in her bed as the very essence of this man set into her soul.

Lela pinched herself to make sure tonight was real. If she wanted to go to sleep tonight a virgin to his touch, she knew she had to get the thoughts of him out of her head. Every five seconds she was on the verge of inviting him to her room. She finally drifted off to sleep with a hearty smile on her face for the first time in six months.

* * *

The next morning, Neil was up at 6:30. He fiddled around in his room and kicked himself for not bringing his briefcase so he could get a little work done. He turned on the TV and started scanning for a movie to preoccupy his time. The only thing on the TV was infomercials and cartoons, so he elected to get dressed. Even though he had only gone to bed three hours ago, he felt like he had a full eight hours of sleep.

Getting out of the shower with his towel wrapped around his waist, he opened the hotel's closet and chose something debonair to wear. There was no doubt that Neil was all male, but when it came to dress and style, some would consider Neil to be metro sexual. He didn't like the use of the term, though. To him, he was just paying close attention to details.

After edging up his goatee, he decided to go to the lobby to grub on the continental breakfast. In the hall, he couldn't fight the urge to stop by Lela's room. *This girl is too damn addictive. Got me at her door at clock nothing in the morning.*

Neil was a serial monogamist; he was always in a monogamous relationship that didn't last more than a year. He had a hard time committing himself to a relationship because of his focus on his career. Every time he would get involved with a woman, they turned into this *boss bitch,* and he wasn't ready to give that title to anyone, so he was definitely out of character to dig a female so deep and so quick like he did Lela.

His last girlfriend, Larna, took him by storm. He couldn't deny that he was in love with her. After two years of dating, the longest relationship he had been in ever, he was prepared to propose to her. That is, until he came home and found her in bed with her best friend and lover, Cindy. Since then, he had been dealing with some trust issues.

Lela had a few things up on his prior girlfriends, though. She had him fiending for more time with her, just to share the same space with her, and sex wasn't the main thing on his mind. Also, Neil had a 'no kids' rule, but Lela could have five kids and he still would be feeling her. The attraction was that deep. Finally, he never ever, ever, ever woke up with a female on his mind. Yet, the only thing he could think about was spending some time talking to Lela this morning.

Standing outside of her hotel room, he knocked.

After a few knocks, he heard, "Just a second." Her sweet voice caused him to smile.

She opened the door with a big white hotel towel wrapped around her. Neil's heart rate quickened as he admired every exposed inch of her smooth skin.

"I didn't know it was you." She blushed and covered herself more. "Hold on a second."

When Lela returned to the door robed, he chastised her on the sly. "Be careful opening the door like that when you don't know who it is. I can't have anything happening to you," he voiced, full of concern.

"I know. I thought you were my mom. She just called and said she and Antwan would be over soon so we could all go to breakfast together."

"Okay, but with all the pretty ladies that are coming up missing, I'd be lost if something happened to you."

"Aww! Really?"

"You can bet that. Your mother and I had the same thing in mind. To take the prettiest lady in the hotel down for breakfast. I stopped by to see if you wanted to go to breakfast, too. I tell you what....I'll get a table big enough for the four of us."

"That would be nice." Lela blushed, thinking Neil must be a playa since he knew all the right things to say.

"Okay, I'll see you down there. And remember what I said about opening these hotel doors," Neil said as he stepped away from the door walking backwards.

"Okay. I will meet you in the café in twenty minutes."

Later that evening, after spending the day at Butts Mill Park in Pine Mountains, Lela and Neil snuck away for drinks in the hotel's lounge.

"So tomorrow I will leave and go back to Opelika, then what?" Lela asked as Neil stroked her long tresses. They were sitting side by side in a booth. She hoped this weekend was just the spark that would light the fire. Though she had been very selective over whom she allowed in her life the past six months, Neil could be the blessing she had been praying for.

"If you're leaving it up to me, then I'm on the highway every chance I get to come see you. We can move as fast or as slow as you want." Neil was never good at beating around the bush.

"How about we put it in neutral and let our friendship, relationship, or whatever you want to call it, move at its own pace?"

"That's a bet." He inched her body close to his and kissed her soft lips.

"Ewww, that's nasty, Mommmyyy." Punkin, Antwan, and some other distant relatives' children were standing by the lounge sofa covering their mouths. Grandma Jana was close behind.

"Come back here, guys!" Grandma Jana said. "I don't know why I volunteered to take all these munchkins to the snack machine at one time."

Lela and Neil laughed, then helped Grandma Jana gather the kids.

"Momma, you like Mr. Neil?" Antwan asked. "My teacher said if you kiss a girl, then you will get her pregnant."

"Oh, boy. Your teacher is telling you too much. Come on; let's get you guys some snacks."

The next day was Sunday, and Lela hated to have to say goodbye to her family. For the first time in years, she had a good time at her family reunion, with the help of a certain gentleman. She knocked on Grandma Jana's room door. She could not leave without some more of her grandmother's wisdom.

"There's my sweet pea." Grandma Jana smiled heartily as she opened the door for Lela.

"Hey, Grandma. I just stopped by to get another hug before I go. I will miss you. Are you sure you don't want to come and stay with me in Opelika for a while?" She hugged her grandmother tight.

"Well, I appreciate it, sweet pea, but your grandma has her own house. I'll be fine." Grandma Jana looked deep into her granddaughter's eyes. "Now, I would be lax if I didn't tell you this, so you listen to your grandma. That guy you've been stuck to all weekend, he's the one."

"What are you talking about?"

"Shy baby. Even a blind man could see that you two are inseparable. I know that the last few fellows you have been with tried to numb it up out of you, but it's called love. Now, when you find love, sweet pea, you keep that tight, and don't let anything or anyone infiltrate what you got. You hear me?"

Lela listened to her grandmother contently. If there was one person in this world whose advice she adhered to, it was Grandma Jana's. "Yes ma'am. I hear you."

"Come here." Grandma Jana patted the spot beside her on the bed. "When you find someone special, someone that treats you like the queen you are, you don't let anything get in the middle of it. Not your friends, work, and definitely not haters. And always, always do the things you did in the beginning to keep him. I don't care if it is thirty years down the road. Do the things that made him fall in love with you in the first place, over and over again. He'll never think of going astray if you heed my words. Keep it tight. Listen, if you think he wants someone else, *you* be the other woman. Richie died a happy man, and we were married for thirty-eight precious years."

Hearing her grandfather's name brought a wave of sadness over Lela, but she let her grandmother's words settle on her mind. "You're right, Grandma."

Grandma Jana smiled her denture grin, and added, "I can tell you really like this one, too, so don't be a playa like your grandma."

Grandma Jana could have taken her act on the road if she wanted to. She was just that humorous, but at the same time she was intense. Whenever she had someone to listen to her, she was never short of something to say to make people laugh, which is why Lela was about to bust a gut laughing at her grandmother's last statement. In the midst of Grandma Jana's sprinkled in comedy, there was always a bigger message.

"I do *really* like him, but I mean, we just met. He seems sincere, open, and to be the perfect gentleman. Plus, he has a great job and some business about himself, but looks can be deceiving. I'm going to take my time getting to know him."

"Well," Grandma Jana winked, "like I said, the best advice I can give you is to keep it tight. Go after what you want and keep it."

"Okay. Well enough about me. When does your plane leave?"

"In a few hours. Calvin is going to take me to the airport."

"Well, I'm about to hit the road. I have to work early in the morning, so I guess this is goodbye."

"Not goodbye...later."

"I love you."

"I love you, too, sweet pea."

Lela promised to call Grandma Jana when she made it home, and Grandma Jana promised to call when her plane landed in

Sacramento. She said her goodbyes to her distant family members, then she and Antwan packed their things to get ready for their trip back home.

She dialed her mother's hotel room. "Hey, Ma. Are you ready to go?" Ms. Rachel rode to Atlanta with her brother Calvin, but was riding back to Opelika with Lela since Uncle Calvin and Dawn were heading to Florida for vacation immediately after the family reunion.

"Just about baby. Give me about five minutes to make sure I have all of my things," Rachel said as she packed clothes tight into her luggage.

"I'll bring my cart around to your room to help you load your things in a minute, okay?"

"Sure, babe. Thanks."

Lela saw Neil leaning on the driver side of her car as she walked across the hotel's parking lot. When he saw her, he rushed to help her with the cart full of luggage.

"Here, little man, let's put these bags in the trunk." Neil handed Antwan the lightweight bags and lifted the heavy bags himself.

"Yes, sir."

"Did you have a good time this weekend?" Neil asked Antwan as the two loaded the trunk.

"Yeah, but I wish we could stay longer."

"Me, too. Me, too." Neil closed Antwan's door behind him and walked back around to Lela's side of the car when what Antwan said struck him.

Taking Lela by surprise, he pleaded, "Stay the week with me in Atlanta. I can get you and Antwan a presidential suite here. That way, we could spend some more time together. Antwan is on summer break, so he won't be missing school." He studied her face, and then added, "Say yes…"

"You've got this all figured out, don't you, Mr. Neil?" She was flattered at his offer, and his begging made it hard to resist. "The offer is very tempting, but I have to get back to work tomorrow."

"Are you sure there is nothing I could say to convince you? I just want to spend some more time with you."

Feeling the need to put some miles between them before things got too heated, too soon, Lela said, "Can I get a rain check?" There was no way Lela would spend the week with him and not get into something deeper than she could handle right now.

Deciding not to push the issue any further, his only response was, "Just say when."

"I will call you when I make it to town."

"If you don't, I'll be in Alabama so fast your head will spin."

Watching Lela pull out of the Hilton hotel's parking lot headed to Opelika, Neil could kick himself for taking his promotion and moving to Atlanta. He wished he was headed back to Opelika behind Lela.

15
Night to Remember

Three months later...

September 21, 2005: It was Lela's birthday, and the 103-degree Alabama heat reflected the hot date she had planned for tonight. When the doorbell rang, Lela rushed to open it. Getting to the foyer, she stopped to check her appearance one last time in the mirror.

Expecting to see Neil on the other side, she beamed as she turned the doorknob. Instead of Neil standing there, it was a delivery man holding the most beautiful arrangement of Peonies. Lela signed for the flowers and thanked the delivery man. She prayed the flowers were a mere preview of what was to come; however, her mood quickly deflated when she read the card.

> *Hey, birthday girl,*
> *The Peony flower means, I LOVE YOU! And this bouquet represents*
> *my love for you. Oh, and this is not your gift. I have much more in*
> *store for you, Ms. James. Sorry that this delivery could not have been*
> *personally delivered by me, but I am caught up again in the office*
> *getting prepared for a major business deal. I will make it up to you!*
> *Yours forever, Neil*

Lela looked at the clock, which read 6:00 p.m. She had already taken Antwan to her mother's for the night, as she was expecting a night alone with Neil. Antwan would be crushed if she were to come pick him up since he had been looking forward to a sleepover with his grandmother.

Lela was not about to spend her birthday alone, though. Therefore, she showered, put on her white lace lingerie set under a slinky red dress, fired up her Jeep Cherokee, and hit the highway.

She had spent the day pampering herself and had even gotten a body wrap, so there was no way she was not at least going to see her man tonight. She realized Neil would probably be working late, but at least she would get to spend a little time with him, maybe even take in a late movie. Over the past three months, she had put some miles on her car driving to Atlanta on a whim and vice versa with Neil. She pondered calling to let him know she was on her way to Atlanta, but decided on a surprise visit.

Since Neil was notorious for damn near spending the night in Naytek, so she stopped by the office first. She pulled into the company's parking garage at 9:30 p.m. and dialed his direct line.

"Naytek Corporation, this is Monica. May I help you?" Neil's secretary beamed.

"Monica, this is Lela. Is Cornelius still in the office?"

"Oh, hi, Lela. No, you just missed him. He said he was going to be working out of his home office the rest of the evening."

"I see. Thanks, Monica." Registering the time, Lela added, "And what are you doing working so late tonight? You are usually out of there by five o'clock sharp."

The two ladies laughed at the truth.

"I would have been gone if Amanda Broady had not placed a stack of work to be done stat on my desk at 4:45."

The secretary used everything in her power not to call Amanda out her name; Lela did the same.

"Well, I pray you speedy fingers to get out of there soon."

"Thanks, Lela. I'm going to need it."

I-20 was jammed packed, so it took Lela an hour to make the twenty-minute drive to Neil's home in Lithonia.

Pulling into the driveway, she flipped open her cell phone and dialed his number.

"Hello," Neil answered in a chipper voice.

"Hey. Open up the garage so I can park," Lela responded.

"Amanda?"

Neil didn't check his caller ID, and only guessed it was Amanda since he was not expecting anyone else.

No, he didn't just call me Amanda, she thought. "Excuse me."

"Lela! What a lovely surprise, baby," Neil exclaimed. "I thought you were Amanda because she just called and told me she was coming over to drop off her last quarter sales report for her clients. That report is due to Mr. Broady in the morning. I was wondering why she would be asking me to open up the garage. That's why I called her name like that." Neil was quick at redemption. "It's open, sweetheart. Come on in."

Now Lela was glad she made the trip.

Indeed, within the hour, Amanda came through with the sales report, and there was one thing Lela did pick up on, and that was the surprise and disappointment which oozed from her pores when Lela answered the door and not Neil.

"Neil is preoccupied at the moment, so I'll take those." Lela gently removed the papers from Amanda's ambivalent fingers, never taking her left hand off the doorknob.

Amanda's visit would be short, and to ensure this, Lela had removed Neil's clothing down to his boxers and was giving him a full body massage when the bell rang.

"Well, I did want to point out this one thi..."

"Go over it in the morning. Good night." Lela slammed the door in her face.

He's in the office twelve hours a day. What is it that she can't say during that time that she has to come over at night and talk about? She must think I'm Boo Boo, the Fool, Lela thought.

"Was that Amanda?" As soon as the front door closed, Neil was standing close behind Lela in his boxers. He relieved her of the reports and placed them on the coffee table.

"Yes, and why couldn't she..."

Neil scooped Lela up into his arms and made a beeline to the bedroom with her.

Between kisses, Lela attempted to finish her sentence. "Give...this...to...you... at...work?"

Ignoring her question, he placed her gently on the bed. After what seemed like an hour of kissing, he took her by surprise when he pulled her dress over her head in one swift motion, revealing the white lacy material that covered her most prized possessions.

He gasped at the site of her.

Lela reached for Neil's blue satin sheet to cover herself, but he caught her hand, taking it in his.

"You're beautiful, Lela. I want to see you."

Over the course of their three-month courtship, he had rubbed every crevice of Lela's body during a few make-out sessions, but this was his first time seeing her unclothed.

"I have waited three months, two weeks, and three days for this moment. I wanted it to come with you as my wife, but I have to have you tonight, Lela. Tonight," Neil said.

Hearing those words, Lela's heart danced to a different beat. She was impressed with Neil knowing exactly how long they had been dating down to the day. *And did he say wife,* she asked herself.

She never knew one word could make her body smile. "I'm yours for the taking. I love you, and even more, I need you, Neil."

To take away any hesitation he may have had, she helped him out of his boxers, tossing them to the floor.

He returned the favor tenfold by removing her panties with his mouth, unsnapping her bra, and claiming her right breast with his hungry mouth as he tossed the bra on the floor. He devoured her left breast with the same fervor.

"Oooh," Lela cried out in pleasure.

Since the time she broke up with Tyrese nine months ago, she had not felt the touch of a man, and there was no way she could hide the desire she had burning deep inside her for Neil. Tyrese had been an expert lover, but what she and Neil shared was different, better. Even she could not understand why she repeated, "I love you. I love you," over and over again, louder each time, as Neil tortured her skin with the feel of his tongue.

She climbed on top of him and caressed his lips gently with her own, making a trail of kisses from one of his broad shoulders to the other. Her tongue delighted in the sensual pleasures that his golden body provided. *He even tastes good. God, I love this man.* Her mind sang a tune of its own.

"If you want me to last, you had better stop that. Remember, I've been waiting the last three months, two weeks..."

"...and three days," Lela giggled as she finished his sentence.

Neil took his place on top of her, showering her face with kisses. "Not that I'm complaining. You are every bit worth the wait, woman," he said between smooches. "Every bit worth it."

Now, it was his time to pleasure her. His lips grazed the nape of her neck and down to her breasts before making a trail of kisses down her stomach to her navel.

Lela's lower lips swelled in anticipation as she writhed on the bed, not sure she could take any more of his sweet torment.

He continued downtown until he reached his destination. By the time his long, wet tongue licked in and out between her legs, the heat from her body formed into beads of sweat that burst from her precious pores. The more she cried out, the more passionate Neil became with kissing and licking her.

Lela clutched Neil's blue satin sheets tight as her legs shook uncontrollably. She was too exhausted to care. For the first time, she experienced a real orgasm. Sure, she had faked them before for the benefit of her ex's, but the shouts of "Oh, Neil. Babeeeee" escaping her lips at that moment were the real deal.

"What's the matter?" she asked Neil, who had slid from the spot he owned between her thighs to sit on the edge of the bed with his right hand on his head and his right elbow resting on his thigh as if in deep thought.

"Are you sure you're ready for all of this, Lela? I know it's a little late to be asking questions, but before we take this next step, let's be clear about it. We said we would wait until we were married."

"Neil, look at me." She struck an 'I'm naked in your bed' pose. "I can't think of a better way to spend my birthday, and you're right, it's a little late to be asking questions after what you just did to me." She flashed him a bedroom grin. "Now, come here."

Neil did as he was told and moved closer to her. "It's just that I love you so much, you wouldn't believe. Hell, I don't even believe it. I have never felt this way about anyone, and I want our first time to be right."

"If this didn't feel right, I wouldn't be here in your bed."

That's all Neil needed to hear. Expressions of their love were sealed with a kiss. He applied a condom and proceeded to make love to the love of his life. He took her with a passion, staking his claim with every blow, as Lela returned his thrusts with the same fervor. She hoped he could feel what her heart felt as their bodies danced to their own rhythm. A series of "I love you...Oh, baby...O...O...O...I'm never letting you go... Whose is it," filled the room until they came in unison.

16
The Infiltration Begins

A side from a few pictures on his desk, Neil did not bring his private life to work. When he entered Naytek Enterprises, he transformed into a no-nonsense businessman. Being so good at what he did, the company's CEO, Christian Broady, used Neil as a model when reprimanding other VP's. His peers told him on more than one occasion that they were tired of hearing, "Why can't you be more productive like Neil? Neil got three new clients last week...Neil this, Neil that."

When it came to the women, there were more than enough beautiful women in the office, but Neil was there for one reason only - business. Accustomed to receiving attention from men of all races, this was one trait Amanda Broady was not used to. Amanda was Neil's latest assignment given by Mr. Broady. He wanted his niece groomed into a shrewd businesswoman, and he knew Neil was the man for the job.

For the third Saturday in a row, Neil and Amanda were cooped up in his office working on an purchase agreement for a smaller software company. She was briefing him on the progress she was making on the Emory project when Neil did something out of character.

"Hey, Amanda, I need a woman's opinion on something." He reached in his pocket and pulled out a small velvet box. "What do you think about this? Is it classy enough? Would you like it?"

"Wow! I know that is not what I think it is. Neil, this is gorgeous." She feigned excitement, then took the ring out of the box and held it in her hand. Before Neil could protest, she had the ring on her finger. "I wish I could be so lucky. Who is the lucky lady?"

Neil gently removed the ring from her hand. The only woman he wanted to wear it was Lela. "Her name is Lela James. Soon to be Lela Johnston, I hope." He replaced the ring into the box. "I hope she likes the ring, but more importantly, I hope she will accept it." It had been a short six months since the family reunion, but Neil was ready to jump the broom.

"She will, Neil. That is a beautiful ring, and what woman wouldn't want to be your wife?" Then, she added with a giggle as if she were joking, but meant every word of it, "Hey, if she won't wear it, I will."

Ignoring the last comment, Neil questioned, "You really think she'll like it?"

"Sure," Amanda replied, and then quickly changed the subject back to work. After seeing the engagement ring, she knew she had to step her game up. Her passive-aggressive approach was not working on him in the least bit.

The final detail of their meeting was bringing Neil up to date on the status of the Emory Hospital and Jacksonville Hospital accounts that he assigned her to work on alone.

Neil gave Amanda pointers on how to better serve her clients, and then they called it a night. He dismissed an unusually talkative Amanda several times before she finally left his office.

They say once you go black you never go back, but when Neil gets a taste of this sweet lily white loving, he will never go black again. Amanda devised her warped plan to get what she wanted. She always did.

17
Ennie Weinny

"Hello." Lela answered her ringing cell phone while coming out of the grocery store.

"Hey, girl, what's up?" It was Tonya.

"Nothing. How about you? I know Robert was over there last night. He must have had you tied up, and that's why you didn't call me back last night."

"Girl, I wish. I don't know how to say it." Tonya tried to hold back a tear which threatened to escape her eye. Her voice was cracking.

Hearing the pain in her friend's voice, Lela stopped in her tracks in the parking lot. Tonya had her full attention. "What is it, Tonya?"

Tonya let it out. "It's Robert. I have been faithful to his *un*endowed butt. I even gave his rusty two-inches the royal treatment on the drop of a dime. Whatever he wanted from me, he got it."

"I thought you said he was packing." Lela was on the verge of laughing about her friend's revelation of the man she had been bragging on, but she thought better of it since Tonya's sniffles and cracking voice corroborated her hurt. Her friend was depressed that she spent the last six months of her life catering to a man that was not her own.

"I thought he *was* the one, all two-inches of him. I was working with him with all of his shortcomings. I haven't been sexed right in six months or more, and for what? So I could snag a rich man, and then to find out *my* man is playing his real woman, and I'm the woman on the side."

"What?"

"Yeah, you heard me right. I'm the sideshow action. He has a wife. Come to find out she is a travel nurse and is out of town during the week, so that's why he is able to spend so many nights with me. That also explains why he gets ghost most weekends. I don't know how I keep getting myself into this kind of drama?"

"Wait a minute…back up! How did you find all of this out?" Lela couldn't believe Mr. Robert's slickness herself. She needed to hear how he pulled this off just in case Neil dared to try this.

"I got off work early today and rushed to the salon so I could look fly for my man. You know how I do." Tonya paused and then continued, "Since he was planning to go out of town this weekend I thought we could spend this evening together. I reserved us a table at La Davio Marina and everything, but when I got to his office at Berk and Taylor he came stepping out of his office with Miss America Wanna Be on his arm."

"I know you went off, Tonya."

"And you know this. I clowned him right on the spot, but ended up getting clowned on. Turned out Miss America Wanna Be is Stacy Taylor, his wife. Why can't I get this right Lela?"

"Don't be so hard on yourself." She thought about her cousin who constantly inquired about Tonya. "The right man is going to come along soon, sis. Meanwhile, do you need an accomplice while we roll on Robert and slice and dice some tires or something? 'Cause just let me know when, and you know I'm down for whatever."

"He's not even worth it. I've written the creep off already. I hope you are right about my day coming soon, though. Because if things keep going the way they are going, I may be crossing over."

"Whoa! Don't get drastic on me. Trust, your day is coming."

18
Make it Official

It was a pleasant spring day when Neil left the office early, heading to Opelika. He could not hold on to her ring another day. It had been four months since he purchased it and they had been dating for a solid ten months since the family reunion. Now, he was sure he was ready to make her his wife. To him, Lela was the definition of beautiful, and not only in the physical state. Thinking back on all of their long talks, long walks, picnics, and whatnots, he knew he had something special. She made his soul sing and beg for mercy, and he truly was at her mercy. So, the fact that he was standing at her door with the tiny velvet box stuffed in his pocket came as no surprise to him. He only hoped she felt the same way about him and would accept his token of love. *Forever.*

He reminisced back to the day they first met. The connection was just there. He knew he was in the presence of someone special because their attraction was so natural. The feeling Neil had when the jeweler presented him with the three-carat diamond encrusted ring was the same connection, so he felt he had the perfect ring for the perfect lady. He could visualize it caressing Lela's soft, beautiful ring finger. Nervousness crept into his spine and threatened to overtake him, but he knocked.

It seemed like it took her ten minutes to answer his knock, but in actuality, it was only seconds.

"Neil, babe, what's wrong?" She could sense his uneasiness, on sight.

He dropped down on his right knee and produced the ring. "Some people say I have it all, but I don't. I'm only a fraction of a man, incomplete, and I won't be whole until I have you with me always."

Lela's eyes did not want to let her grasp what was going on. Neil was proposing. She stood there with her mouth wide open as if frozen in time.

Neil continued his plea. "I have the house, the car, money, and plenty of friends. Yet, I don't have you *with* me. Lela, I'm asking you, will you complete me? Will you? Will you be my wife? Will you be Lela Carla Johnston for the rest of your life?"

When the words finally released from her throat, she replied, "Yes, baby, I will." The words sprang out, along with a river of tears from her eyes.

Rising from his kneeled position, Neil hugged her tightly, picking her up off the ground. "I love you so much, Mrs. Johnston. I am going to take good care of you. You will not regret this day."

"I know I won't. I love you, too, Mr. Johnston."

"Mom, is everything okay?" His mother's crying had Antwan scared.

Neil flashed a wide grin. "Little guy, everything is just perfect. Your mom and I have some good news."

Later that night, Lela stood in the foyer holding the door open while she talked to Neil who stood right outside the door. "Do you have to go?"

"If I didn't, I'd still be curled up on your love seat with you."

"Well, soon, Antwan and I will be in Atlanta with you and we won't have to spend any time apart, because as soon as you leave, I get lonely."

"Babe, it tears me up when I have to get on that highway without you."

"You want me to move in tomorrow?" Lela joked.

"Hell, you can come tonight if you're asking me, but I know you want to get Antwan set up in school first."

"Yeah...I did say that. I have to take care of my little guy first, but I need to take care of my big guy, too."

"You're doing a good job of taking care of me, believe that." Neil took Lela into his arms for a heated kiss.

Two hours later, he finally left for Atlanta.

19
Treachery Knows No Bounds

Buzz...Buzz...Buzz. Neil's hand fumbled around, successfully hitting the snooze button of the alarm clock on the nightstand. Allowing his head to sink back into his fluffy cotton pillow, he hoped he could pick back up on his dream in which Lela was serving him a four-course meal at a table fit for a king. He had just gotten to the part where she was standing in the door of a secluded cabin wearing a French maid's costume. He closed his eyes and snuggled up close to the pleasing body beside him.

The warm body lying beside him, in his bed, almost felt real...too real. Was it possible Lela had come to him in his dream?

His lids felt like they were being held together by a cement block, so it took him a few seconds to focus. Opening his eyes, he winced in pain. It felt like he had been hit by a sledge hammer. The alarm blared out once more, and again, he pressed the snooze button. *8:01 a.m.*

"What the..." Neil rolled over and rubbed his eyes vigorously. What he was seeing could not be real. The curly blonde hair sprawled out over his black silk pillow scared him shitless at first. He sat up ready to throw some blows with the intruder.

When he realized who it was, though, he lay back on his pillow and closed his eyes. Surely when he opened them, the unclad, perfectly tanned, and strikingly gorgeous woman, whose sexy legs were intertwined with his naked body, would be gone. Surely, Amanda Broady would not be lying in his bed. Surely.

"Amanda?" He shook her vigorously like he was attempting to

awake the dead. "Amanda, get up."

"What is it, baby? You ready for round three?"

Round three? Oh…hell no!

"What's going on here? How the hell did you get in my bed?" Ashamed of his own nakedness, he jumped to his feet and scrambled through his bottom drawer for some sweat pants. *How the hell did I get naked,* he questioned himself over and over.

"After a night like last night, don't play dumb. You are magical, babe, but I knew you would be."

"Play dumb? Magical." Amanda's bedroom eyes pierced into Neil like an omen. This was a side of her he had never seen. He became sick to his stomach. "This can't be happening."

He rubbed his throbbing head, trying to make some sense of it all as he rambled off what he could remember of the night before.

"You came by last night when I got back from Opelika, and you had champagne. That's about all I can remember." *Lord, tell me I did not have sex with Amanda last night. Tell me, Lord, please.*

Neil pleaded for a sign that Amanda lying naked in his bed was some sort of twisted joke and the punch line would soon be delivered. When he made it back to Atlanta from Lela's place last night around 12:05 A.M., Amanda was waiting on his doorstep. He was in good spirits because the love of his life had accepted his hand in marriage, and he and Lela spent the evening consecrating their engagement.

Although iffy about Amanda's late night visit, he invited her in nonetheless. She claimed there was something she *had* to tell him that could not wait until morning. He remembered her holding a bottle of Moet, and at the time, he was so exhausted he didn't bother to question why she had champagne.

Amanda offered him a glass of Moet in celebration of his engagement, their accomplishments in the office, and as thanks for him being a great mentor. He could recall everything except when things went fuzzy after he drank the glass of champagne. He could only hope that Amanda had not thanked him too properly. Having sex with Amanda would have been a miracle anyway, considering Lela drained him of all the energy he had earlier that night. He could barely make it home he was so tired.

Having relations with Amanda was bad for business and triple as bad for his personal life.

"You must have had too much to drink because you knew very well what you wanted last night, and it wasn't what's her face…Lela."

Amanda confirmed what Neil had been silently praying against. Her face was decorated with a devilish grin. "I will gladly take her place. She doesn't know what to do with a man like you anyway. You need a woman of my style and grace. Plus, the way you took me last night, I would have thought you hadn't been sexed properly in years."

"Take her place? Amanda, listen, this…" He pointed to the romantic scenery of champagne glasses, sheets nearly hanging off the bed like some real bumping and grinding went down there, and Amanda in her birthday suit, though ever so sexy. Her creamy tanned thighs commanded his attention all the way up to her bikini-waxed twat with a heart-shaped patch of hair above it.

Lela's picture on the dresser stared back at him erasing any fleeting attraction he may have had for Amanda. It was as if she were in the room daring Neil to look at Amanda's naked body again.

He continued with his back to Amanda. "This never should have happened. I am in love with Lela. I just asked her to be my wife, for Christ sake."

He racked his brain once again. *Surely there is a logical explanation for this,* he thought. He never had a problem holding his liquor, so, as much as he wanted there to be, there was no explanation fathomable for whatever led to Amanda spending the night in his bed.

"I am sorry for whatever happened, but this is where it ends. Now, if you will, please get your things and leave."

She sprung toward him, grabbed his arm, and forced him to turn around so that they were face to face. Her D-cup breasts sprang wildly about. "You bastard! I thought what we shared was special. How dare you throw me out like the morning trash?" Her voice was full of hurt.

What we shared? Neil's stomach tied up in knots when she said that. "To be honest, as far as I am concerned, we did not *share* anything. All I remember is having a drink or two with you last night. The rest is a blur. So, as far as I am concerned, there was nothing. No-thing. Now let us be civil about this, and not say things that we will regret later. "

He gathered up her belongings and handed them to her. Spending an unwanted night with the young, white niece of his CEO could be career suicide, so Neil made an attempt at self redemption. "If we are going to continue to have a successful business relationship, it is best we put this behind us, Amanda. We both know this is unprofessional. If you would like another mentor, I understand totally and will oblige. I could get Sandy Pearson to work with you."

She put on her sweater and jeans as quickly as she could. When she finished dressing, she got in Neil's face as she ranted. "Always the proper one, aren't you, Neil? Well, you can keep your idea about Sandy Pearson mentoring me, because *you* are going to continue to be my mentor and whatever else I want you to be." She pasted on an evil grin. "I want you for myself, and I won't let you off that easy. You are going to continue to work with me *and* give me what I want when I want it. If I'm not happy, then your little fiancé definitely won't be." She laughed, "Hmph. I'll teach you to use me, and then we will see who regrets what."

"First of all, I don't take kindly to threats. Secondly, I did not use you. How could I have used you when I don't even remember inviting you into my bed? That should tell you something right there. I'm a one-woman man, and that woman is wearing my ring."

"But she's 200 miles away, and what she doesn't know won't hurt her." Amanda flipped the script as she rubbed her hand up his back.

Neil stepped away from her clutches. "I will know."

He led her to the front door and opened it. Neither of them knew what to say next. Amanda spoke first.

"From the way you took me last night, looks like you need a backup plan anyway. I wonder how precious Lela would feel knowing I may have Neil Jr. before she gets the chance to. Yeah, lover man, you were all up in this raw. Now sleep on that."

Neil shivered at that thought. "You're wearing on my patience. If anything, you took advantage of me. Now, you need to get the fuck up out of my house before my job is the least of my worries."

Seeing she was pushing him over the edge, she softened up. "Neil, I'm sorry. I would have never come on to you if I did not think you were in your right mind. I thought you wanted me to. We can put this behind us, but I will never forget how special last night was to me." Her voice sounded sincere.

"Bye, Amanda." Neil motioned his hand for her to walk on through the front door. At that moment, it would not have mattered if she walked in front of a speeding car.

Amanda stepped outside of the door. "What happened here is between the two of us. Deal?" She extended her hand, and when Neil accepted it, she pulled him into an embrace.

Unlike Amanda, Neil did not notice Lela standing in the corridor observing their exchange. Amanda had been a busy little bee. At 5:00 a.m., Amanda called Lela and told her that she needed to get to Atlanta ASAP because Neil was acting disoriented. She convinced Lela to come immediately to check on him. She knew Lela showing up at his house in time to witness her leaving with a sleepover bag would be the trick to rid them both of Lela.

He poked his head out of his door to see what had Amanda's attention.

"Lela?" He walked past Amanda, wishing he could pull a Houdini and make her disa-damn-ppear.

He hugged his, he hoped, soon-to-be wife, giving Amanda a '*you ain't gone yet*' look.

"Uh...she was just leaving." It was as if she needed this cue to move her feet.

"Hello and goodbye, Lela. Yes, I was leaving."

It was not until Amanda smirked at her that Lela spoke to Neil. "I see that, but I guess my question is why is she *here* and looking like she's been here all night." Then to both of them she asked with sarcasm, "What'd y'all have a sleepover?"

"I got into a huge fight with my uncle, and Neil was kind enough to let me sleep on his couch. Neil really is the only person I have to talk to in Atlanta since all of my friends are in Tennessee. I was going to rent a hotel, but he was kind enough to let me stay here. Completely innocent. Trust me, you have a good and faithful man. I called you this morning because he was talking in his sleep and I could not get him to wake up. Turns out it was a false alarm." She put on an act so good, she almost believed herself.

Lela didn't buy it, though. "I see." Then to Neil, she said, "I came because Amanda called me this morning and told me you were disoriented. I don't want to intrude on you helping out your friend. You both seem to have been there for each other last night."

The tension in the air was thick enough to cut with a knife.

Coming over to her man's house to find him standing in the door shirtless and hugging a disheveled Amanda was one thing. It was Amanda's pink overnight bag that threw her for a loop, especially when this particular woman spends more time with her man than she does already. The same man who professed his undying love for her the night before. The same man whose ring she was wearing. All of these factors were bringing the bitch right up out of Lela. Feeling it would be best to remove herself from the situation, she did a 180 degree turn and headed back to her car.

Oddly enough, Amanda was still standing in the doorway like she had a right to. Neil wasn't a violent man, but he thought he might kick her throat in if he didn't have to go chase Lela down.

"No, baby, don't go!" He practically pulled Lela inside of the house and closed the door in Amanda's face.

He ushered Lela over to the loveseat.

"No, I will stand. What's really going on? And don't give me any lame excuses either, because I'm not new to this. I recognize the game when I see it being played."

Neil scratched his head. It was best he came clean, which is exactly what he did. He told Lela everything he could remember of how Amanda came to spend the night in his house. The part about them ending up naked in his bed and Amanda claiming they had butt-naked sex all night long, he left off.

★ ★ ★

The next morning, Lela decided to pay a trip to Naytek Enterprises to mark her territory. Neil was putty in her hands, and making sure that fact was one hundred percent clear to Amanda would be vindication enough for her. She considered a beat down, but she had to play the part if she was to be Mrs. Cornelius Johnston, VP of Operations at a Fortune 500 Company. She couldn't go barging into his firm and start a fight with the president's niece.

"Neil, Lela is here for you. Do you want me to escort her in?" Monica spoke into the intercom.

Lela noticed Amanda peering through the blinds of her office after Monica had spoken her name. *That's right. I'm here to show you that I'm the top lady in Neil's life, at home and at work.*

"Yes, please." Neil's voice brought an instant smile to Lela's face and the mention of Lela's name made Neil's heart melt. Amanda had tried, but did not succeed at infiltrating their love.

"To what do I owe this honor?" Neil asked, taking the oversized brown bag from Lela's hand.

"You have been working so hard, I thought I would bring you lunch."

"Mmmmmm. You know Outback is my favorite, but you didn't have to come all the way from Opelika to bring me lunch." He rubbed his stomach while hungrily eyeing the bag.

"I got you a T-bone, medium well. Just how you like it."

"You know what else I like?" He crossed the room quickly and pulled her gently into an embrace. "I like this, and I love this." He kissed her neck before kissing her lips ever so tenderly.

"You know I can't take that kind of torture. We're up in this office, too. You're going to mess around and have your employees getting an earful."

"Don't threaten me with a good time." He called her bluff, closing and locking his office door. Neil then pulled his lover back into his arms and allowed his hands to interrogate every inch of her body.

Lela kissed him with a passion she had only known for him, and somehow, the Altoid on her tongue ended up in his mouth.

"Mmmmmm," he repeated, enjoying his most delicious pastime, kissing Lela. He picked her up off her feet and into a tight embrace.

She wrapped her arms around his neck and her legs around his waist.

"Wait," Lela reasoned with him. "You know I can't be quiet, and I'm not going to be walking out of here embarrassed."

After sucking her bottom lip and then her top lip a few more times, Neil gave into Lela's warped reasoning. Even though he wanted her right then and there, he allowed Lela to slide to her feet.

"Forget my employees. I'm the only person in this office you have to worry about pleasing."

"And I intend to." Lela sashayed over to his desk to retrieve the goodies she brought for him.

Neil clapped his hands together and tilted his head to one side as he enjoyed the view in front of him. Lela was dressed, revealing yet classy, in her blue two-piece mini skirt set.

She prepared his desk for their lunch with him sitting on the opposite side. He repositioned her settings, bringing her directly beside him. He craved her body heat and wanted her closer. When she didn't give in to him sexually, he wanted her even more.

While feeding one another, Neil did not keep his hands off of her. He allowed his hands to roam freely over her thong-clad derriere. His body was rock hard at this point.

"What are you trying to do to me, coming in here like this?" Neil whispered low in her ear. "I mean, really." There was no doubt in his mind that no other woman could shake a stick at Lela. She ignited his fire without even trying. Just watching her eat turned him on.

"What?" Lela played dumb. She knew exactly what she was doing.

Finished with their meal, Lela cleared and rearranged his papers back on the desk.

"You need to stop your mess, Mr. Johnston. I need to get back to Opelika to get some shopping done before I pick up Antwan. Plus, you know you have work to do, so I'm not going to keep you tied up."

"Well, while you are shopping, buy something sexy for tonight."

"Tonight?"

"Yes. I'll be at your place by five, and then by next week, I want you and Antwan moved in."

"Antwan has two more months before school is out, and I have two more months to get our wedding together, so we will have to hang in there. Until then, I will have a lot of miles on my car."

"And so will I."

"Secondly, don't you worry your savvy little head about what I'll be wearing tonight. Have I ever disappointed?"

"No, you never disappoint, except for coming up in here starting something you're not willing to finish," he teased. "As far as work, it's a wrap. I'm leaving behind you." He looked around his office as if someone had brought him at gunpoint to Naytek and he was attempting an escape.

With her purse on her shoulder, she straddled him while he sat in his desk chair. "Bring that appetite to Opelika and it's on."

He kissed her one last time before letting her out of his sight. "Oh, I'll be there. Nothing is going to keep me from getting my fill tonight."

<u>**20**</u>
Those Who Wait

"That bitch!" Amanda slammed down the Emory customer feedback forms. "What is she doing here? I thought after yesterday she would have been history."

Amanda tried to clear her head and pretend Lela was not in the office next to hers probably seducing the one man she wanted to be with more than anything. She picked up the feedback form from the Human Resource manager at Emory. *Excellent service! Neil and Amanda were the perfect duo…*, the manager wrote.

Amanda picked up the company newsletter so she could see his picture, the same one she kept on her nightstand beside her bed at home, and said, "too bad he can't see that we would be invincible together."

Amanda's scars were still evident from Kent walking out on her. Her husband of five years left her a 'Dear Jane' letter and with Neil's rejection all of those memories came rushing back.

Dear Amanda,

We've both known for a while that the love was gone from our marriage. It has gotten to the point that we are both just going through the motions. I can't live like this anymore. I'm tired of living a lie and Carey is tired of sharing me with you. I will not fight you on keeping the house and I have left you half of the money in all of our accounts. Make the best of your life. There will be someone out there for you. We just were not meant to be.

Best wishes, Kent

Amanda remembered leaving message after message on his cell

phone. "Damn you and your whore, Kent! I didn't deserve that. All I ever did was cook your meals, clean your drawers, and keep myself a perfect size 6 so you would love me. Why did you have to do this to me?" She wept right on her office desk as she reopened her old wounds.

Neil's moaning and Lela's giggling resonated in her office that was adjacent to his. "Neil…why are you doing this to me? *Why?* You're just like Kent."

Amanda went to her office restroom and ran some water over her face. She popped two of the pills her psychiatrist prescribed for depression and walked out into the reception area to give Monica a new assignment. About the same time, Lela strolled out of Neil's office readjusting her skirt.

Amanda overhead Neil say, "…Nothing is going to keep me from getting my fill tonight." Amanda's envy had to be showing on her face when Lela sashayed out of Neil's office like she was on top of the world.

Back in the confines of her own office, she could feel his tight embrace around her. It had been Lela's name he was calling, but he was caressing her body two nights ago.

We'll see who gets the last laugh. You will have your day to squirm, Lela. Amanda always gets what she wants, and Neil is at the top of the list, sweetie. When I'm done with you, you'll slither away in shame.

Amanda face turned up in a satisfied grin. She decided she would lay off a little with her advances toward Neil for the time being. Especially after spending a night in his bed without his consent.

Even though he was not fully aware of everything that had been going on, lying there in his arms felt right. She knew she had to get her mind right. Having to see his heavenly body, listen to his sweet voice, and smell his seducing scent day in and day out would be difficult, but she would bide her time.

Good things come to those who wait.

21
Etched In Stone

It was June, 24, 2006 when Neil and Lela tied the knot. She wanted a quaint, small ceremony, but Miss Rachel and Zora, Neil's mother, ended up inviting over five hundred guests. They moved the wedding to Zora's church, Greater Tranquility Baptist Church, a mega church in downtown Opelika.

Tonya was the maid of honor, and NaQuetta served as the matron of honor. Their fuchsia strapless dresses fit them to perfection. Trey was the best man, and Mark, Neil's friend from college, served as the only groomsman. Antwan was the ring bearer. Lela absolutely glowed in her silky white gown with sheer and lace flowing train when she came floating down the aisle.

Speaking from his heart, Neil vowed, "Lela, you are the reason I get up in the morning and the sedative that puts me to sleep. Since I met you one year ago today, my life has taken on a different perspective. Sharing this day with you, being here with *you,* makes this moment bigger than life. I know it is right. Everything about you is so right. When I met you, I wasn't even looking for love, but what I found in you was a fountain of love. I have never loved anyone the way I love you. I vow to be everything you need, want, and desire from this day forward. You have my heart, forever."

With tears pouring from her eyes, Lela was able to give her vow to Neil.

"Neil, it's every girl's dream to be in love and get married to a wonderful man. You have shown me the true meaning of love and what a good man is. Before you, I did not have the definition of a good man. You changed that for me. Today…"

She raised a manicured finger to her eye to wipe away her free-flowing tears.

"Today, all of my dreams have been realized. When you walked into my life one year ago today, you stole my heart. But today, I give you my soul. I vow to be everything you wish for in a wife and to fulfill all of your needs and wants. I will be by your side until death do us part. I'm yours, forever."

The deal was sealed with a breathtaking kiss.

Amanda had the only dry eyes in the place. She sat in the back pew on the groom's side, rolling her eyes. The whole display disgusted her. She felt she should have been the woman at Neil's side. She did not think Lela had the grace it took to be with a man of Neil's stature.

The reception hall was decorated simple yet elegant with rich cream table coverings, a bouquet of fuchsia roses centering each table and fuchsia and cream balloons adorning the walls. The lighting was dim and votive candles were placed strategically about the room. On the banquet table, there was a lighted beverage fountain, an ice sculpture and a huge spread of exquisitely prepared finger foods.

Miss Rachel outdid herself with the decorations and catering. She covered every detail, making sure her daughter's day was perfect. She offered to keep Antwan in Opelika with her for the summer since it was summer break and Antwan would not be returning to school for three months. That would give the newlyweds some much needed time alone.

The offer sounded sweet to Lela, but she couldn't swallow being separated from her son for an entire summer, and neither could Neil. However, Antwan's pleas to spend the summer in his hometown where he could visit his old friends won Lela over.

"Okay, but I'm not promising you the whole three months. I may come and pick you up early, so don't be surprised," she told him.

After the first dance, cutting of the cake, countless pictures, and spending a few hours with their family and friends, Neil and Lela made an escape to the airport, where they caught a plane to Jamaica, eager to get the honeymoon started.

22
Honeymoon Surprise

People say honeymoons last the first year, and so far, that was panning out to be true for Lela and Neil. The first two months had been breathtaking. They were like magnets to each other. With Antwan spending the summer with his grandmother, they had the opportunity to spend every moment together in intimacy. Neil worked at home as much as possibly, and Lela made it her business to cater to his every need.

For the past week, Lela woke up sick to her stomach and hurling into the toilet. She didn't think much of it because there was a nasty stomach virus going around the community, and she could have picked it up at any one of the functions that she and Neil attended together in the past month.

After returning home from her annual Pap smear exam, Lela called her friend with some unexpected news.

"You won't believe what I found out at the doctor today."

Tonya responded blasé saying, "well, don't stress me out with waiting. What?"

"I'm having a little Neil." When Tonya didn't respond, Lela repeated, "I'm having a baby. Can you believe it?"

"Oh, I can believe it. The way you two have been going at it, you barely have a few minutes to pick up the phone to call your best friend," Tonya spoke in monotone.

"Try not to sound so happy for me," Lela said sarcastically.

"You know I'm happy for you. Jamaica must have been really good to you. Juicier than what you told me. "

"A married woman never tells her business," Lela schooled her friend, "...but girl, just know that we had to order a new frame for our bed last week."

The two friends laughed.

"I'm not even going to chase that one. Listen now, don't go turning into an Old Maid now that you are pregnant. You know how you did with Antwan. If anyone ever acted like they couldn't bust a grape while they were pregnant, it was you. You wouldn't even comb your hair most days," Tonya reminded her friend. "You just got married. You got to keep on giving it up like you have been and keep the diva alive, even in pregnancy. I hate to see pregnant women who let everything go because they're pregnant."

"Spoken like a woman who has never been pregnant."

"Whatever. You don't have to cut me down like that. You know I want kids."

"You are going to have one soon, Tonya. I can feel it. I had a dream just the other night about fish."

"That was for you, silly."

"No, it can only be for me if someone else dreams it."

"Oh," Tonya simply replied, not a bit superstitious.

"Well, I'm about to go pick up Antwan from school. I just left Neil's office giving him the good news, so you were next on my list to call because I knew you'd be happy to hear you were having another godchild."

"Yes, girl, I'm happy for us. I've got me another baby to spoil."

"Talk to you soon. Oh, and Tonya, I miss you, girl."

"I miss you too, Lela. I miss having a road dog."

"I'm going to have to come down there before I get too big so we can have a girl's night out and hit up The Foxy Lady for old times' sake."

"Just let me know when, and I'll come get you if you want me to."

"Sounds like a plan. I'll talk to you later."

"Kiss Antwan for me, and take care of my goddaughter, too."

"So you think it's going to be a girl?"

"I don't think, I know."

"Let's hope so."

23
New Beginnings

Tonya was the first to arrive for Lela's surprise baby shower. Rachel had Lela preoccupied shopping, giving Neil, Tonya, and Trey enough time to get the bash together. At seven months, it was a hard task to get Lela to leave the house, but a surprise visit by her mother did the trick. Lela jumped at the offer to spend a day shopping with her mother, like old times.

Antwan opened the door before the first ring.

"Hey, little man." Tonya swept him off his feet. "Where is your dad?"

"Hey T Tonie!" After hugging Tonya's neck tight, Antwan giggled and pointed in the direction of the kitchen. "He's in the kitchen cooking for my mommy's party."

Tonya walked into the kitchen with Antwan by her side, holding his hand.

Neil and Trey were busy slaving in the kitchen. Neither noticed Tonya's entrance.

Trey donned an oven mitt to remove a pan of hot wings from the oven, when he turned to see Tonya standing there in a sweater dress and leggings. Her hair had fresh micro braids with dark ringlet curls flowing down her back. Standing there with his mouth open, Trey's oven mitt fell to the floor.

"Hello, Tonya." Trey crossed the room to stand in front of her, and noticed Antwan looking at his godmother with dreamy eyes.

"Antwan, you got to get your own woman." Trey teased his little cousin and kissed Tonya on each of her cheeks.

Jealous, Antwan wiped both of Tonya's cheeks and said, "This is myyyyy T Tonie." He then landed two of his very own sloppy kisses on her jaw. As far as he could remember, he had always been Tonya's number one little guy.

Trey turned to Neil, who had quietly watched the exchange, and said, "Look at the little Mack Daddy, Neil. You training 'em right. He knows a quality woman when he sees one."

"You need to quit, Trey," Tonya said coyly.

Neil turned to observe the couple. They now had his full attention.

"Antwan, we have our work cut out for us, buddy. Go and watch the new Shrek 2 movie I got you," Neil told Antwan. Then to the lovers he said, "As for you two, we have to get all of this stuff done before Lela gets here, so keep your hands to yourselves."

"I'll try," Trey said as Neil carried some meat out on the patio to the barbeque grill.

As soon as the coast was clear, Trey pulled Tonya in for a long fiery kiss, caressing every inch of her backside that he could reach.

Coming up for air, he said, "I missed you."

He took his hands off her hips and waited for her response.

She released her breath from her throat. She felt like she had not breathed since she first saw him drop the mitt on the floor. He took her breath away every time she saw him.

"I missed you, too, babe."

After bumping into each other at Charlie's Seafood Station last night, the lonely hearts connected and shared a night of passion, and even more this morning. The few hours they had been apart they missed each other immensely. They could no longer fight their attraction.

He took her by the hand and walked her into Neil's study that was a wing off the kitchen. Neil would be back in the kitchen at any second and he wanted to sneak a few minutes alone with Tonya.

"So you don't have any regrets about what happened between us last night and this morning, do you?"

"Should I?"

"No. I plan to be your man. I'm ready to settle down. I just need to know where you stand. You *are* looking for a man, right?" He was not ready to put his feelings all out on the line without knowing where Tonya's head was at on the matter.

Tonya blushed. "Let's take it one day at a time, okay?" On the surface, Tonya could mistake him for being insincere, but deep down she knew that he meant every word.

"Oh, this feeling is going to last. You just leave that up to me. I've got a few tricks up my sleeve." Trey turned back around and motioned with his hand for Tonya to lead the way back into the kitchen.

"That's what I'm worried about, the tricks up your sleeve."

He grabbed her around her waist from behind, pulling her back into the office.

"As long as you are with me, you don't have anything to worry about."

He kissed the nape of her neck. She could feel her body respond in ways she would rather it not, given their locale. She closed her eyes to savor the feeling, though.

"I love you," escaped her lips.

Hearing her words caused her to open her eyes wide with surprise. She wasn't cognizant as to whether she actually said them aloud or not, but when Trey turned her around to face him and kissed her hard on the lips, her fear was confirmed. She had told Trey she loved him.

It was true. She felt love for him, but she hadn't planned on telling him so soon. Having been friends since they were kids, she always liked Trey, but *love*?

She let her thoughts go and allowed her body to enjoy what Trey was doing to her.

"I love you, too, Tonya."

The shocked expression on Lela's face when she walked in the house to find all of her friends and family in her house for the shower was priceless. She received so many gifts that she and Neil only had to purchase a crib to be ready for their new arrival. Neil's gift to Lela was a fully decorated nursery; he chose neutral colors because they wanted the sex of the child to be a surprise.

On April 10, 2007, ten months after the wedding, Jalan Cornelius Johnston graced the world with his presence.

Part 3

Struggles Between Good And Evil

24
Exhausted Desires

With her two-year wedding anniversary only a month away, Lela was starting to feel the zest dwindle down to zilch in her marriage. A lot of married couples she knew said they went through the same thing, but going through it yourself is an eye opener. She never thought there would be a day when she and Neil would not talk each other to sleep. Or a day when they would not want to rip each other's clothes off, even after an argument, especially after an argument.

Yet, lately, Neil was so caught up in his work and spending so much time working with Amanda, he didn't have the energy to deal with Lela or the kids at the end of the day. The fact also remained that two years into the game she was still dealing with Amanda's antics. This past month alone, Amanda had managed to go on two business trips with Neil, have five business dinners with him, a couple brunches, and quite a few late nights in the office, with most of those meetings being the two of them alone.

Amanda called the house constantly, sometimes at the oddest hour, and always with a new revelation about work. Something that magically slipped her mind in the office, but became super important late in the evening. There was nothing Lela could say to clue Neil in on the inappropriateness of it all. She would have thought after the incident a few years back where Amanda ended up staying the night at his house that he would be hip to what Amanda was up to, but alas, Neil remained an Amanda apologist.

In the midst of it all, insecurity had crept in on Lela in the worst way. Not because she felt inadequate compared to Amanda, but because she couldn't get and keep her man's attention for more than five minutes. He was so into his work lately. She knew he was a workaholic from the get go, but his hours and time away from home were getting ridiculous.

In the mornings, Neil rushed off to work, so most mornings he was gone before she awoke to dress the kids for school and daycare. He spent his nights late in the office, and then stayed up even later in his home office when he got home. That was if he wasn't out of town on business.

Neil and Amanda took more business trips together in an effort to tag team the company's larger clients. Naytek's advances meant a decline in the unity in the Johnston household.

In the beginning, Neil went on his business trips alone. Now, Amanda was working in his shadow more and more, and Lela was getting uncomfortable with their closeness, especially since Amanda stopped by the house almost nightly intruding on the little quality time their family had together.

Even though Neil was oblivious, Lela picked up on Amanda's demeanor around her husband. Deep down, she thought Neil would not betray her by sleeping with Amanda, but the more time Amanda spent in their lives, the more suspicious she got.

Neil had been preparing for a large account he wanted to score. The account would add five million dollars in revenue to Naytek per year. He would get a one-percent bonus if he secured the account and a one-percent per year residual bonus. Therefore, this was a big deal for him financially and professionally.

Lela helped him prepare presentations and role played as he recited his sales pitch. He was really working hard on this account, and she wanted to do all she could to help him, but getting this account meant he worked from seven in the morning until sometimes eleven or twelve at night. When he did finally make it home, he was either too irritated or tired to deal with anything else.

Tonight, Lela watched her worn-out husband working diligently in his home office. She walked over to the back of his chair and massaged his back.

Turning his chair around to face her, she said, "Neil, you have been working all day. Let's go to bed together tonight for a change."

"I'm coming. I just need to check one more thing."

"That's what you always say." Lela turned and walked out of his office. She saw no need in arguing because work would win.

After an hour of working at his desk, Neil fixed himself a cup of juice and went to his room to take a shower. When he stepped out, Lela had his towel open, waiting to dry him off. As she towel-dried him off, she kissed his back around to his lips.

He took her into his arms, hugging her tightly and kissing her hungrily.

Lela purred, "Let's get in bed."

Neil pulled Lela down onto the bed on top of him and said, "Let's just lay here and enjoy this moment."

Before Neil's head hit the pillow good, he was snoring.

Disappointed, she kissed his cheek and rolled off him.

"Goodnight, Neil."

Even though Neil was giving his best at being more attentive to Lela's needs, her insecurity about Amanda and Neil was taking its toll. Lela lay awake listening to his snores bounce off the walls until she finally drifted off to sleep.

The very next night, Lela rolled over and looked at the clock, which read 12:45 a.m. *I need to get some sleep,* she said to herself as she lay there with her thoughts once again.

She tossed in the bed and took in the caramel brown smooth skin covering his masculine frame. She had her own GQ model lying in bed beside her. She thought of the day she fell in love with him. It was the moment down to the second and hour that they saw each other at her family reunion three years ago.

Her love for him to this day was not in question. There was no denying that. She could never love or respect another man more. After all, he was the man who put the ring on her finger, a father to both of her children, and the one who held her heart.

With all that said, she also had mixed feelings about what she was going to do with the rest of her life besides be Mrs. Johnston. Neil being so consumed with work and having not touched her in weeks left Lela second guessing her decision to quit transcribing and doing the homemaker thing.

If I'm not going to be getting any attention at home, at least I could work, she thought. Quite frankly, she was bored with the whole 'Neil's wife' title being the only definition for her life. She felt she had lost herself somewhere in Neil's world.

She had few friends in Atlanta. NaQuetta moved down there a few months ago after Lela told her how much money could be made by opening her own salon in the ATL, and Tracey was a girl she met at the gym, but they were just acquaintances. Furthermore, her friends had lives, and Lela didn't want to intrude on them with her problems.

For the first time, she was starting to feel an emptiness she could not explain. *Midlife crisis,* she wondered, but being only thirty-two, she ruled that out for the time being.

Her thoughts kept her conscious when she desperately needed to sleep. *I remember the good ole days.*

It was ironic, but now those days seemed to be when she was out running the streets with her girls looking for a good man. She shook her head, thinking it would jar some sense back into her, because no matter how depressed with her situation she got, there was no denying that a damn good man lay in the bed beside her.

It became a ritual for Lela to lie in bed and think about how much fun Tracey and Tonya, who were still swingers, were having. How exciting their lives were. They constantly had some juicy stories to tell her.

With her being married, she was not about to discuss her husband's skills with them. Then she thought, *Maybe I don't have anything to talk about because nothing's going down in the bedroom. Aside from not paying me one bit of attention, he's not giving me any loving, and I refuse to beg.*

Neil had not initiated sex in the past two months. Every time they had been together sexually, she made the advance on him. So, for the past week and three days, there had been hardly any conversation and definitely no sex, which left Lela to her devices.

As much as she wanted to be supportive of his career, she wished Neil would be a little more attentive to home. Or at least be a little more spontaneous. Screw her brains out, at best. She could start her own reality show: *The life of a horny housewife.*

At this point, she would settle for just a little spontaneity in her life. His idea of "spending time together" was him sitting on the sofa with her with his laptop in his hand while she watched a movie.

It was a battle between good and evil going on inside her head, and the evil was winning.

I mean, this is all good, but sometimes I just want to hang out with people my age, drink, and enjoy life. Hell, I'm only thirty-two. If

I can't get it at home, don't mean I can't get it. The evil voice continued its rant. *They say thirty is the new twenty.*

Her good conscious kicked in, reminding her of all his good attributes and explaining to her that trials don't last always. *You promised to be by his side through thick and thin. Hang in there.*

Her eyes were now fixed on the clock, which read 1:15 a.m.

Neil was all that a woman could ask for, a tall dream lover with a smile that could melt butter. He brought home the bread, too, banking well over $250,000 a year. So, his hard work and long hours were paying off tenfold. He made it possible for her to be laid up in a 4,000-square-foot house with a three-car garage, pool, and Jacuzzi. She lifted a finger at nobody's job in the last two years. Housekeeping came on Fridays to help with housework. The landscaping was immaculate in front of their upscale private-gated lakefront community in the Pointe Shores area of Lithonia, Georgia. Beautiful hills surrounding the community with the calm blue water of Lake Thurmond were the centerpiece. Gorgeous large oaks and dogwood trees added to the beauty of their new home. Whenever at home, he did help Lela with the kids. He loved the hell out of her and was faithful. What more could a woman ask for?

Some sex maybe, she thought. Thoughts continued to flip flop in her mind. *I'm losing it.* She tossed and turned over to face Neil.

Neil turned over in his sleep and threw his arms around her waist, pulling her head into his chest. He held her close and fell back into a deep slumber with her in his arms.

Lela exhaled. *I'ma work on the issue of him not paying the kids and me enough attention, but aside from that, I can live with this.*

She smiled and finally drifted off into a deep sleep.

The next morning, Lela woke at 5:30 a.m. to the sound of her alarm. She hit the snooze button, hoping she could get in ten more minutes of sleep; however, Neil getting out of bed stirred her out of that thought. Surprised he was still home, she watched him walk to the bathroom.

"Morning babe," she mumbled half asleep.

"Good morning doll."

Within minutes, Lela's tired eyes closed and she drifted back off to sleep.

25
All Work, No Play

Lela set the dinner table for three. Neil had just called and informed her that he would be in after dinner *again*. Lela decided against waiting for him since the last time she did that it was after 10 p.m. before he made it home. She placed her steaming hot homemade dishes on the table. Baked chicken. Stewed potatoes. Fresh field peas. Cornbread. For desert the boys would enjoy Oreo cream pie.

While preparing the table for her incomplete family, Lela was in deep thought. She could no longer keep her thoughts silent, so she spoke out to no one in particular. She was alone.

"How is it that a man whose attention you crave so much and who was so attentive in the beginning just let things dwindle down to nothing? He must be getting is somewhere." Lela's dark conscious snuck in and articulated her worst fears.

She quickly suppressed the thought, and told herself, "he's just working late. I have to give him space to accomplish his goals." She reminded herself of what Neil always told her. "Hard work today will pay off tomorrow."

Lela and her sons enjoyed a perfectly prepared meal and talked about everything under the sun from *Blues Clues* to *Spiderman*. As she was tucking them into bed at 9:30 she heard Neil come in. She met him in the living room.

"Hey babe," Neil kissed Lela making his way to the kitchen

discarding his tie and dress shirt along the way.

"Is there another woman? Just tell me Neil."

Neil gave Lela a confused look. His eyes told her that he was too tired for the drama.

"I know you and nearly two weeks without sex is just not you." She did not and could not believe that he would cheat on her but at some point reality and common sense had to kick in.

"First of all, I left a pile of work on my desk to come home to my family. I was sitting at my desk unproductive because all I could think about was you and my sons. I had a lot of work to get done, but when I looked into your eyes in the picture on my desk all I could think about was coming home and having dinner with my family, helping Antwan with his homework and tucking Jalan in. Do you think I like working so many hours?"

"Well I guess I should feel honored that you are *thinking* about me, but I need you to *be* with me. And you still didn't answer my question."

"That's because I shouldn't have to. Look Lela, I don't feel like arguing tonight. I just want to eat my dinner, shower and hug up with you until I fall asleep. I need to get some rest before I have to get back on the grindstone tomorrow and I refuse to stay up all night arguing over nonsense."

"Fine then." Lela placed Neil's plate on the table and poured him something to drink. "Let's start over. How was your day?"

Lela and Neil retired to bed soon after dinner and a little conversation. The next morning while brushing his teeth, a sumptuous image caught Neil's attention. The mirror gave a perfect reflection of Lela's toned brown legs.

He had been working so hard lately, he didn't realize until that moment what he had been missing at home. When he did want to be intimate with Lela, she was busy caring for the kids. One of the things he admired about her was her attentiveness with their children. But with the kids still asleep, Neil saw the perfect opportunity to steal some quality time with his wife.

He turned around and leaned back on the sink for a minute to enjoy the view, admiring every bit of his wife's beautiful body. Lela's silk gown had inched up above her waistline, exposing her bare skin. She was all his and he wanted to slap himself for missing out on nearly two weeks of not making love to her.

Ever since giving birth to Jalan, Lela constantly worried about losing weight, but Neil couldn't think of one inch of her that he wanted to part with. She had fuller thighs and her booty was more to hold on to. The more he mesmerized over her, the more his body responded. Walking over to the bed, he stood above her for a moment just taking in the sight before him.

All work and no play ain't working out for a brother, he thought. Neil then picked up his cell phone from the nightstand and called to leave a voicemail message for his secretary, letting her know not to expect him early and that, in fact, he may be running an hour or two late.

Next, he removed Lela's head scarf to reveal her silky black straight hair. She looked like an angel in her sleep. One of his favorite pastimes was watching her sleep, which made him remember back to when they first started dating. Before they had ever been intimate, he knew he wanted to marry her after holding her asleep just one time in his arms.

He eased the covers back and slid into the bed, placing kisses down her spine. He worked his way back up, leaving no skin untouched. Stopping at the nape of her neck, he kissed her long and tender there. This was her spot, and he knew, if nothing else, this would wake her.

When she turned over and kissed him, his heart melted into hers.

"Good morning, babe," he said when she broke their kiss.

"A good morning it is," she replied as she wrapped her arms tightly around his neck.

"You miss me?" Neil caressed her thighs. He slid his hand in her lacy panties, massaging her gently.

"So much you wouldn't believe, but uh...I'll be right back," she said above the beam of her smile.

Lela eased out of his grasp and got up from the bed. If she wasn't dreaming, she wanted it to be perfect. She eased into the bathroom to freshen up before giving him time to protest. Her gaze and swagger let him know she was just as hot as he was.

"Come on, babe. Don't worry about that."

"Give me just a second, babe." Once in the bathroom, she looked to the ceiling and thanked God for answering her prayers last night. She didn't know how much more neglect she could take.

Neil took the time that Lela was in the bathroom to lock their bedroom door. He would hate for their little morning escapade to be invaded by the kids.

When Lela came out of the bathroom, Neil was now sitting up on the side of the bed.

"You know you didn't have to freshen up for me. I love to love you no matter what. The good, the bad, and the ugly. Morning breath and all. I may not tell you this enough, but you are beautiful." Neil wrapped his arms around her waist and hungrily placed butterfly kisses all over her neck.

"Do go on," she said, relishing in the compliments. "But how do you know that I wasn't trying to give you a hint, hint?"

Neil tackled her playfully onto the bed. "Oh see, I'ma have to make you pay for that." He used his mouth to untie her robe and discovered she had left her gown in the bathroom. "I see you know what time it is."

"And what time is it, Mr. Johnston?"

She licked her lips, revealing the hidden pleasures that only he knew lied within. They kissed for what seemed like an hour until she could feel his swollen body about to burst through his boxers.

"I can show you better than I can tell you."

"I think I'm going to be the one showing you. Get ready to be sucking your thumb on the way to Naytek today," Lela bragged.

He snatched her robe off in one swoop and kissed her from her toes all the way up to her inner thighs. When he reached her thighs, he licked a trail up to her midsection gently kissing and sucking her body. When Lela's body shook, releasing her pleasures in between moans, he kissed his way up to her belly button.

"Neil! Please don't stop. Oh...my...God. I...missed...you!"

He lowered his head back between her juicy legs, placed two fingers deep inside her, and continued his tongue assault, bringing her to a second climax.

"I love you, Neil."

Neil looked into Lela's pleasure-ridden eyes. "I love you, too, baby." Neil took pride in satisfying his wife.

He picked her up off the bed. "Come here."

"What are you doing?" Lela asked anxiously.

He slowly backed her into the wall, placing her up against the wall with her legs wrapped around his torso.

"What's that you were saying about me sucking my thumb?"

"Mmmm." She moaned long and soft as he entered her. He thrust in and out of her, making her climb the wall with each stroke. Her body was consumed with so much pleasure, she couldn't move. All she could do was quiver and look deep into his dark brown eyes.

"Neil! I love you, Neil! Neil!"

His strokes were long and hard, like he was confessing his love for her with every movement. He claimed her mouth again and tongued her down, never missing a stroke.

"Oh shit, baby! I'm coming!" she screamed, covering him in her juices. He released right after her. Even though Lela had been up in the clouds three times, Neil was just getting started. While still inside her, he returned to the bed and sat down. He lay back on the bed with her atop of him. No intermission necessary.

Just to think, last night, Lela was complaining about getting no affection, and now she was trying to think of a clever way to get out of this predicament she found herself in.

Neil cupped her breasts and sucked them until they were sore. She moaned, enjoying his painful pleasure. By this time, she was moving her hips and loving him properly. "O...baby...O. This feels so good." She moaned and moaned.

"You like that?"

"Uh huuuhh!"

"Move slower, Lela. I want this to last forever."

She did as told and put her knees down on the bed, slow grinding like she was getting paid for it.

Now it was him who was professing his love to her. "I love you, Mrs. Johnston! You feel so good."

She climaxed again, and when he felt her muscles contract and her juices flowing, he released what seemed like a year's worth of sexual frustration. Too tired to move, she laid on his chest in a state of euphoria. Lela did not know what had gotten into Neil this morning, but whatever it was she wished it would visit more often.

"I'm sorry for not being the man I should be around here, lately. I don't want you to think it's because I don't crave you. Lord knows I do. It's just that I'm making major moves at work, and when it is all said and done, we're going to be pretty well off." He turned her face to his so that he could look at her. "I know you get lonely and feel deserted sometimes, but it's far from that. I am here for you, forever. Just know there is a light at the end of the tunnel."

They laid there intertwined until they heard a little knock at the door. It was Antwan. They only hoped their early morning escapade was not what woke him up.

"Ahem. Sounds like you woke the kids up, Neil," she teased.

"Don't even try to put it on me. That was you screaming and sucking *your* thumb, mind you."

"Just a minute," Lela responded to the small pitter pattering on their bedroom door.

She tied her robe tightly around her body, and Neil slipped into his pajama pants, kissing her one last time before unlocking the door.

Antwan ran in and jumped in the middle of the bed.

"What's the business, little man?" Neil asked, rubbing him on the head.

"Nothing much, dad. Good morning, momma," he kissed his mother on the cheek. "What was all that noise in here?"

They looked at each other with devilish grins.

"I don't know. Go brush your teeth and start getting ready for school," Lela told him, kissing him on the forehead. "And wake Jalan up," she added on his way out of the master bedroom.

"Momma, are you going to have a baby? I heard you say 'O, baby'."

"No, there's no baby. That was the TV, Antwan," Neil lied.

"Your clothes are hanging on your closet door. Go on and start getting ready babe, I'll be in there in a minute." Lela kissed Antwan on the cheek.

"Okay momma, I will."

"I'll see you before I go to work, little man."

After Antwan disappeared from the doorway, Neil kissed Lela again.

In a soft whisper, she chastised, "You are wrong for lying to Antwan like that. He's smarter than he looks."

"He looks pretty smart to me. Give me another kiss."

After Lela had gotten the kids ready for school, she sat at the breakfast table with Neil.

"I'm going to go to the beauty salon today and get my hair cut. Do something different with it. Add a little spunk."

"Baby, I like you just the way you are." He laughed and hit her on the butt with the newspaper. "But if you want something different, go for it. Just don't come up in here looking like Keisha."

She laughed. "Oh, I won't, trust," she replied as she took some grape juice out of the refrigerator.

"Just be looking good for me when I get home tonight. Keep it tight for me."

"Don't I always?" Lela giggled.

As he walked out the front door, he called to his sons, "Bye, boys."

She looked forward to looking good for him so they could pick up where they left off this morning. Reminiscing on how she felt last night and then the festivities of the morning, she sent up a silent prayer.

Thank you, Jesus. I know now why I love this man. When they say ask and ye shall receive, there is not anything more true. You always send little reminders to let me know how blessed I am. I pray that my family stays together. Lord, thanks again!

26

Natural Beauty

A fter Lela dropped Antwan off at school, she drove forty minutes to Marietta to get her hair styled. Neil agreed to get off in time to pick up the children, so this gave her extra time to go to the spa after leaving NaQuetta's shop.

"NaQuetta, I want you to hook me up with some highlights, a nice short cut, and maybe one of those Mary Kay facials, too."

"Okay, cool. So you want the Halle Berry look, huh?"

"I wish. Nah, nothing like that, just hoping a change on the outside will help keep my spirits up. I've been stressing lately and staying up late. And then, you know I have to look good for my man."

"Yes, you do. Where is that fine man of yours anyway? I wish I had a man who would let me stay at home while he worked and took care of me the way Neil does. Heifer, you better count your blessings and watch yo back!" NaQuetta joked.

"You know I've got my back, front, and sides covered, so watch your mouth, chick. Don't get cut up in here. You know I don't play about mine. I'll put a heifer in a choke slam in a minute!" Lela blurted out in a mixture of joking and dead seriousness with NaQuetta.

Having been friends since high school, they always had each other's back and were down for anything, especially when it came to their men. If they ever caught one another's man out cheating, they had no problem confronting him and his date for each other.

One time, NaQuetta confronted Lela's ex who was walking hand in hand with Trina, a girl they couldn't stand. He didn't know what hit him when NaQuetta straight cursed and spit at him for cheating on her friend so blatantly in public. Then, she dared Trina to act like she wanted to jump in it.

Lela and NaQuetta carried on for the next two hours, talking, laughing, and exchanging jokes about old brawls for old time's sake. They were cracking up laughing about the good old days when NaQuetta spun the chair around and said, "You like?"

"Girlfriend, you outdid yourself!" Lela said thankfully. "Like it? I love it." She started singing, "I got my hair did, I got my hair did." Then returning to being serious, "Now, do my facial, using just earth tones on me. Don't try anything erotic on me. I wanted to tell you last week that facial you did on Keisha was jacked up. I don't want to look like I'm joining the circus, just accent my nat-u-raaaal beauty," Lela said, sashaying around in her chair.

"Keisha?" NaQuetta laughed. "I did that on purpose." She smirked. "That's what she gets for running around in the hood talking about me. Done told all my little business that she picked up on when she was in the shop. Like these streets don't talk."

They both laughed together. "Girl, you are a straight up G then, huh?" Lela said jokingly.

"Nah, that's you, dog. Married with kids, and still a G."

Lela finished getting her facial and eyebrows arched, then gave NaQuetta a big hug after paying for her new look. Her next stop was Fancy Nails.

While looking at her watch as she exited the salon, she bumped into Terrance Moore, an old flame she never really got a good fire started with. When their eyes met, Lela started tingling and felt a hot flash come over her. The feeling made her visibly nervous.

Whoa, the years have been kind to you, she thought. She averted her eyes away quickly.

He recognized her right away and spread his arms, bringing her close to him. "Hey, Lela! Long time no see."

"Hey, Terrance. How have *you* been?" she said, emitting a flirtatious aura.

"Good now that I ran into you. You damn sure looking like you've been doing just *fine!*" He raised one of her hands in the air and walked 360 degrees around her, eyeing every curve on her body.

"Yes, and I see you're still a big flirt."

He grinned, showing his dimples and a smile she was all too familiar with. "Yeah, you always could bring it out of me. I stopped in to get an edge up. You see a brother's jacked up right now."

"No, you look good to me," she blurted out before she knew it.

"So where are you headed?" he inquired.

"Oh, I live in Atlanta now. I have a few more errands to run, and then I'm heading back home."

"You got a minute." He looked at his watch. "There is no one ahead of me, so I should only be a few minutes. I would like to take you to lunch, if it's okay with you?" Noticing her reluctant body language, he pleaded, "Just to chat for old time's sake. Please don't turn me down."

"I don't think that would be a good idea," she replied reluctantly, holding up her ring finger to show her wedding ring set.

"There's a lucky man somewhere for sure. You *are* all that."

She hit him on the shoulder playfully. "Boy, stop!" Then once she saw that he had taken her words seriously, she added, "I'm just kidding. Do go on."

"There you go with your sense of humor. Bet you think I forgot how you used to make me laugh. It's too bad I got beat to the punch."

He looked her up and down, sizing up the new Lela. Ten years had passed, and she still was beautiful. Better than he remembered. Deciding to step up his game, he thought of anything he could say that would get her to spend more time with him.

"I can respect that, though. It will be completely innocent. Just lunch with an old friend."

Lela looked around, hoping an answer would drop from the sky. She didn't have any plans for the afternoon except to go home and do some housework, but that could wait. Neil was picking up the kids. Her mind was telling her, *hell to the no*, but her body was saying, *yes, yessss, go to lunch with this young, fine, creamy chocolate Hershey specimen of a man.*

While looking around, NaQuetta caught her attention. NaQuetta's eyes were bucked and she looked like she had something sour in her mouth. She mouthed the words "no way" and shook her head, warning her friend of the impending danger.

Lela looked back at Terrance with all intentions on saying 'no thanks' when, "Yeah, sure. What could it hurt?" came floating off her tongue. She was a big girl and had her feelings in check, so really, what could it hurt?

"Great. Give me about five minutes, Lela."

Lela sat in the waiting area of the salon wondering what the hell she was doing waiting on her ex. *Are we going on a date? No way! Just catching up with an old friend. Neil would understand,* she told herself.

She and Terrance had an intimate, but nonsexual, relationship back in college. It was not nonsexual because of lack of trying, 'cause they had tried several times. But he was so huge that she could not handle his size, so the furthest she ever got with him was third base. There is nothing that drives a woman crazier than thinking back on an old flame that could have been much more.

They dated on and off for about a year when their relationship finally fizzled out. They both attended Floyd State University, and even though they both were engrossed in their coursework, it seemed he was the one that rarely found time for her. She would call and call some weekends, but he wouldn't be available for one reason or another. When he rarely made the initiative to contact her, she decided to give up on their one-sided relationship.

NaQuetta approached Lela with her blow dryer in hand.

"I know you are not waiting on Terrance?"

"Yes, and before you ask, we're just going as *friends* to lunch together. Nothing more." Lela hoped NaQuetta would drop the subject.

"What the hell are you thinking? You're a married woman, and he is your ex-lover." NaQuetta walked around so she could face Lela who had turned away from her.

"If it's *just lunch,* then why are you standing there looking like a schoolgirl after having her first kiss?" She raised her eyebrow, waiting for an answer, and when Lela didn't respond, she said, "The man is your ex for a reason."

"It's just lunch with a friend," Lela said sternly.

"Be careful of the webs you weave. Remember, I told you that on this very day. Write it down, take a picture, because I have a feeling we are going to revisit this issue again."

"Quetta, you worry too much. I can handle myself. I love my husband, and no man is going to get in the way of that."

"I hope you know what you're getting into."

"I do. Now, go wash Sheila's perm out. She's over there fanning like her head is on fire."

"Oh shiznit! I forgot about her." NaQuetta rushed over to her client who was vigorously fanning her head. "Call me when you get home, Lela."

"I will."

27
Eye Spy

Lela trailed Terrance to Chili's Restaurant in her Jeep. Seeing him step out of his blue Chevy Tahoe with cream leather interior, she got nervous. Old feelings that she buried away a long time ago came rushing back into her system. She thought about cranking her car up and heading home to Neil who should be at home any second now with Antwan and Jalan.

She could kick her own butt for agreeing to have lunch with him.

Inside the restaurant, he held out the chair for her to sit down and took a seat directly beside her.

"What are the odds of me bumping into you on a day like this, Lela?"

"I don't know. What kind of day is it?" Lela said as she fidgeted in her chair, adjusting and then readjusting her black skirt.

"A day when it seems everything else is going wrong. Seeing you is the only good thing that has happened to me today."

Before Lela could find out what was going on with Terrance, a bubbly waitress walked over to their table and placed a menu in front of each of them.

"Hi. Welcome to Chili's. I'm Amy. Can I start you out with something to drink?"

"I'll take a Budweiser." Terrance had the rest of the afternoon off and was looking forward to winding down.

"A glass of water, please." Lela knew she had to keep sober in order to keep her mind right.

"Would you like to try one of our delicious appetizers?"

"No, thanks," Terrance answered.

Sensing her inhibition, Terrance tried to lighten her up when the waitress walked off to get their drinks. "I know you better than that. You sure you don't want a daiquiri or something?"

"Thanks, but no thanks. I have to take my son to a baseball game tonight, so I need to keep it together."

"You...a son? I wouldn't have guessed that you had kids. How many do you have?"

"Two sons."

"That's good. Really nice." He raised his right eyebrow suggestively and added, "Maybe I'll get a chance to make you one of my famous strawberry daiquiris one day. You fell in love with those back in the day."

"I don't think so." Moving right along, Lela asked, "I know you're a big time businessman somewhere. Where are you working?"

"I run a publicity firm."

"Moore Publicity 4 U?" Lela guessed. She heard of the black-owned company before, but never knew Terrance was the brains behind the operation. "I should have put two and two together on that one. You always said you wanted to get into the business side of Hollywood."

"Yes, that's me."

"I'm glad for you. I really am," she said in between sips of her water that Amy placed on the table.

Reaching to touch her hand, he said, "I know I said this would be an innocent lunch, and it will be, but I can't let you out of my sight without telling you how much I still think about you and how much I wish things would have worked out differently between us. Back then, I was struggling trying to finish school, but I really wanted something with you. I was not really experienced in the relationship arena. Now, I know how to take care of a lady. I would have loved for that lady to have been you. In fact, I have been trying to get NaQuetta to give me your number for at least a year, but she said you were happy and to leave you alone."

"Yeah, NaQuetta is protective of my marriage to Neil. That's how friends do." She eased her hand out of his grasp, and held up her ring finger. "As for everything else you said, that would have been all that I wanted to hear three or four years ago, but now, I'm happily married."

"Yeah, but are you *really* happy?"

"Very."

"I can't compete with that, can I? I shouldn't have ever let you go when I had my chance, but that's neither here nor there. So let's just enjoy our meal and this time we do have together."

Lela was relieved to hear that. For a second, she thought she would have to leave him sitting there. Three years ago, it would have been a different ballgame, but she had a man who loved her and whom she loved more than life itself. She was not interested in rekindling anything with Terrance.

They spent the next hour talking about everything under the sun. Afterwards, Terrance tried convincing Lela to meet with him again. He even invited Neil to come along with her if it meant he would be able to see her again. Needless to say, she politely refused his offer.

On the other side of the restaurant, unexpected eyes watched Terrance and Lela's every move while snapping pictures with their digital camera. *Well what do we have here? Mrs. Johnston has a little dirty secret herself. One day, your world is going to crumble. Don't worry, maybe your new man will pick up the pieces, or maybe not. I could care less.* The self-appointed investigator laughed and continued to snap the valuable shots.

When their lunch was over and she was standing at the door of her Jeep saying goodbye, Terrance gave her a friendly hug and snuck a kiss.

"Terrance, don't do that! Don't make me think coming to lunch with you was a mistake."

"I'm sorry. I couldn't resist."

"Well, you can't be doing that. I am…"

"Married. I know."

"Take care of yourself, Terrance." Lela hopped in her vehicle and turned the key in the ignition.

Standing in the parking lot, Terrance watched Lela until she drove off. "You, too, Lela."

While pulling into her gated community, Ice Cube's "Today Was a Good Day" came on the radio and she grinned. She made hot love to her husband that morning, got a makeover, and had lunch with an old flame. *Today was a good day,* she thought.

28
Midday Treat

Two weeks had passed since Lela had lunch with Terrance, and he had not crossed her mind. Only when Neil went on hiatus from his husbandly duties and focused strictly on work would Lela wonder what Terrance was up to.

Her alarm went off at 5:30 a.m. as usual, but she snoozed until 7:00. She barely made it out of bed in time to get Antwan off to school. She piddled around the house in a sleepy euphoria. Despite her daze, she managed to get Antwan to school by 7:45. With a virus going around at Jalan's daycare, Lela kept him home all week. For the life of her, she could not understand why the daycare would allow children to continue to come while they were sick, and then act surprised when other kids in the center came down with the same sickness.

Jalan fell asleep in the car on the ride home. Lela was glad to see her son sleeping peacefully, because after her long night with Neil, she had hoped for a nap this morning, too. After pulling into the garage, she got out, carefully removed Jalan from his car seat, entered the house, and took him into his bedroom. He was sound asleep when she tucked him back into the bed and headed to her room.

She took a hot shower, put on one of Neil's oversized t–shirts, and dove into her bed. Lela was glad Neil left early today so she could get some sleep. All this week, he had been putting in overtime keeping her satisfied. Not even five minutes passed before she was fast asleep.

An hour later, the phone rang, waking her out of a deep slumber.

"Hello," Lela murmured groggily.

"How's my sweet pea? Sleep?" It was Miss Rachael's cheerful voice.

"Hey, Ma. Yeah, I was sleep. What time is it?"

"It's almost nine o'clock, but I was talking about Jalan."

"Nine o'clock? Why you calling so early? Is everything okay?"

"Because I thought you would be up with Jalan. Now, how's my grandson?"

"He's doing good. He went back to sleep after we dropped Antwan off. Usually I would be awake, me and him both, but today we slept in."

"Well Jalan is the reason I was calling. I want to pick him up and spend some time with him today. Mr. Jesse drove me down to Newnan today to see my neurologist and we decided to make the trip on up your way. I was thinking about taking him to The Ice Cream Factory for an ice cream cone and then to Keisel Park."

"That's fine. What time you coming?"

"I'm outside your front door now."

"Maaaaaa!"

Lela hung up the phone and went to the front door to let her mother in. Her mother was notorious for her surprise visits. For the next hour, Lela and her mother chatted while dressing Jalan. He was too excited to be going out with his grandmother, who would no doubt spoil him rotten.

"Have a good time, sweetheart." Lela kissed Jalan on the cheek.

He returned a big sloppy kiss to her on her lips and flashed a big cheeseburger grin. "K. Me wit nanny."

"Ma, try not to spoil him too much."

Rachel winked at Lela. "We'll be back before it is time for you to leave to pick up Antwan." She looked back at her daughter, who looked exhausted, and was glad she came. "Oh, and make good use of your time alone."

"I will, Ma. Thanks."

When her mother pulled off, she let her last words linger. *Make good use of your time alone.*

Lela walked through the foyer and into the living room. All of her housework was done. Watching TV was out; she wanted to do something more than sit in front of the tube all day. She watched so much TV since she stopped working that everything on would probably be a rerun to her anyway. She thought about going to the spa and salon, but she planned to do that with Tonya on Saturday.

After a long relaxing bath, Lela wrapped herself in her pink terrycloth robe and stepped into her walk-in closet. She turned on the light, and after spotting her clothes sprawled out all over the floor, she had a flashback of what Neil started last night.

She knew exactly what she was going to do. She was going to have lunch with Neil at Naytek. She dressed in a black mini-skirt and crochet top, slid into her black sandals, and hoped he would not be too busy for his midday surprise.

★ ★ ★

Neil ran his hand across his low-cut curly hair. He was exhausted. Between the long night with Lela and having to come in early this morning, he contemplated leaving at noon. He flipped through his itinerary and was glad he did not have any afternoon meetings. Picking up his phone, he dialed Amanda's extension.

"Amanda, could you come to my office, please?"

"Sure, Neil, just a sec."

Amanda entered Neil's office less than a minute later. "You wanted to see me?"

"Ah, yes. Were you in the middle of something?"

"No. I was reviewing the satisfaction scores from our new clients. Nothing that can't wait. What's up?"

"Very well. I want you to get ready to take on your first mega million-dollar sale alone, completely solo. I have worked with you over the past few years and have seen a lot of growth in your negotiation ability. I think you are ready for this one. Christian and I have been chomping at the bit on this one for a while, and he and I both think you can finish the deal."

Amanda smiled, taking in all of her compliments with grace.

"The client is Richardson Norcross Memorial Hospital, and they are interested in outsourcing their entire medical record department."

"The entire department?"

"Yes, even the clerks would be on our payroll. They are pretty much sold on the idea that we can offer them the same service they have currently at a twenty percent cost and overhead decrease. We have already given them the names and numbers of some of our current clients who are happy with our services, and Richardson Norcross is pleased with the feedback they have gotten from them so far. They have a good feel for what they can expect from Naytek, and what we will provide has been documented in their file. All that is left for you to do is close the deal and squash any concerns they may have during the transition."

Amanda had an apprehensive look on her face, and Neil picked up on it.

"I have been working with you, grooming you for the big league. As a result, Christian and I think it's time to clip the wings, let you fly. You have done well on the clients you represent thus far. You have to believe that if I didn't think you could do it, you would not be. All you have to do is put your qualities to work that you have been working since you've been at Naytek and enjoy your bonus check."

Neil's smile weakened Amanda's apprehension.

Amanda walked over to his desk in tears. "Thanks for having so much confidence in me. I have never worked with anyone as kind and genuine as you."

Neil walked over to her and handed her a tissue from his desk.

"I'm sorry to get so emotional. I guess I'm having one of my 'need a hug' moments. I really meant what I said about you being genuine. You are the most genuine person I know." Without warning, she hugged him close.

Neil had not seen this side of Amanda, and hoped not to see it again any time soon. He couldn't understand why this cut-throat business woman he had seen reign in and out of the boardroom was crying. Now, she would be able to close her own deals without his assistance. Two-and-a-half years is plenty on-the-job training, and if he had it his way, she would have had her own assignments two years ago. However, she always came up with a reason or two why she needed to continue to work under him, and would convince Christian that she needed the extra time to train.

Neil reluctantly returned the awkward hug.

★ ★ ★

Lela stepped off the elevator and was greeted right away by Monica.

"Good morning, Mrs. Johnston. You want me to buzz your hubby? He's in his office."

Lela put two fingers over her lips and shook her head no. "Let me surprise him." She noticed Monica was glowing and said, "you look great. Your new hairstyle is absolutely beautiful."

"Thanks." Monica rubbed her jittery hand through her spiral

curls. "A girl named NaQuetta did it. She has a shop over in Marietta. Here, I have her card if you want it."

Lela cut her off. "No, I know exactly who you're talking about. Quetta is my girl, and my stylist, too. She knows how to do some hair."

Lela looked across the hall toward Neil's office. "Well, look, let me go steal some time with my man. As always, it was good seeing you."

"Okay. Take care, Mrs. Johnston."

Lela waved her off. "It's Lela. Every time I come in here I ask you to call me Lela."

"I always forget."

Neil's door was halfway closed, so Lela eased the door open slowly and peeked in. If he was busy, she would not barge in on him. When she got the door open wide enough to peek inside, her euphoric mood went out the window.

She heard Amanda say, "I have never worked with anyone as kind and genuine as you." Then Neil and Amanda locked up in each other's arms in a way that was a couple levels past employer-employee friendly. She stepped back and made sure she had the right office. *Yeah, the door says Cornelius Johnston, Vice President.*

Neil didn't notice her come in until she slammed the picnic basket down on the table beside the door.

Lela tried to calm herself, but her voice was filled with attitude. "Neil, did I *catch* you at a bad time?"

Neil swiftly stepped away from Amanda and made it to his wife's side. He planted a brief kiss on Lela's lips and held her hand.

"No, of course not. I've always got time for my number one lady."

Number one lady? So is he suggesting she's number two? Lela's mind was working overtime, and the smirk and extra pep in Amanda's step had her blood boiling. Lela used every nerve ending in her body to suppress her ghetto twin *Lelaquisha.*

Amanda, who was obviously pissed that Lela broke up her affectionate moment with Neil, had a hard time hiding her jealousy. She ignored his wife's presence, looking right past Lela. "Neil, do you still want to go over the specifics for the new client?"

Never taking his eyes off Lela, he replied, "I will go over all the details with you before I leave today. I'm probably going to leave shortly after noon anyway."

With Amanda still standing there, Neil added, "You'll have

plenty of time to start your research. Meanwhile, go over those satisfaction scores, and you can brief me on those as well when we meet later."

"Do you want to go over them at lunch?" Amanda asked, even though she saw the picnic basket.

"No, definitely after lunch. It looks like a pretty lady has taken care of lunch for me." He smiled as he met Lela's unreceptive gaze.

Amanda walked to the door with her head held high, pretending to be unaffected by Neil's obvious devotion to his wife. It was too late, though, because her face expressed more words than she ever could, and 'pissed off' was written all over it.

"Okay. I'll see you later," Amanda said as she walked out of his office.

Neil closed and locked the door behind Amanda. Before he could get a word out, Lela was all over him.

"Neil, what are you doing hugged up with that bitch. You know I don't play that."

"It was nothing, Lela, nothing. She got her first mega client today, and she became emotional. I handed her a tissue and she hugged me. I didn't want to be rude, so I just patted her on the back a few times. That's when you walked in."

"Well, what was she talking about when she said you are the nicest and most genuine person she has ever worked with?"

"That's because I am. You know that, but I treat everybody that way. Monica would tell you the same thing. Baby, stop being so insecure." He wrapped his massive arms around her waist and tried to assure her that his heart only belonged to her.

"I trust you. It's not you that I'm worried about, so much as Miss Amanda and her plans for *my* husband. And the fact that you spend so much time with her is not comforting in the least bit."

"I know. I know. If she does well with this client, she will be rolling solo from here on out."

"Well, maybe that's why she was crying then."

"I'm ready to dive into what you brought me. We rarely get moments like this, so let this time be about me and you. Not Amanda."

"Okay. I'm letting it go for now, but know this. I'm *not* you're number one girl. I'm your *only* girl."

"Oh, and you bet that. The one and only, so stop being so touchy."

"I'm not touchy, I'm worried is all."

Neil guided her into his arms and rubbed her back gently. His hands moved gently down to her legs and back up under her mini skirt. "Is that what I think it is?" He referred to her not wearing underwear.

"You like that?"

Neil picked Lela up, and she wrapped her legs around him. He kissed her like a long-lost lover. Neil was glad Lela chose her outfit well today, and leaving the panties at home was plain genius. "I'll let you be the judge of that."

He was so aroused he couldn't take another second without making them one. He laid her down slowly on his sofa, removed his pants and entered her eagerly.

Both pleased and aware of her surroundings, Lela whispered into Neil's ear, "Baby, please…don't…make…me…scream."

He covered her lips with his to smother her screams. At that moment, he could not understand why Lela felt she had a reason to *ever* be jealous of another woman. It was crystal clear to him that he would not be leaving her for another woman ever.

"What are you doing to me, girl?" he said. "I'm about to come. I swear, if you move your body like that one more time, I'm going to explode."

Lela moved her body vigorously as she felt her peak coming. She matched Neil stroke for stroke. With their lips locked to stifle the noise, they climaxed together.

Neil kissed his wife and fell back on the leather sofa. He ran his finger up and down her legs, admiring her skin.

"Come on." He picked her up and walked to the restroom connected to his office. After they both washed up, Neil unlocked his office door, and they sat and ate the chicken salad sandwiches, pickles, and grape juice that Lela had prepared.

"I heard you say you were leaving early, so I'm going to get out of here so you can wrap your day up. I'll be at home waiting for you. Antwan has a game tonight, so you will get to go with us for a change."

"I wouldn't miss it. I'll be out of here in about an hour. "

When Lela walked out of the office, Amanda was chatting with Monica at the receptionist desk. Lela was sure Amanda had at least a clue of what was going on behind Cornelius Johnston's closed door, and had no problem with it.

"Goodbye, Mrs. Johnston. I mean, Lela," Monica said with knowing eyes and a pleasant smile on her face.

"Goodbye, Monica. See you soon."

Lela cut Amanda a sharp eye and pressed the button for the elevator.

While stepping into the elevator, Lela heard Amanda say to Monica, "Like what was that for?"

"I don't know." Monica shrugged her shoulders.

29
Interception

Later that week, Neil was sitting at his desk putting the final touches on the Emory proposal. He and Amanda stayed in the office late last evening working on the proposal, so all it needed was polishing for his nine o'clock meeting with Christian.

Just as he pulled up his itinerary for the day, his secretary buzzed. "Mr. Johnston, just a reminder of your nine o'clock meeting with the board. It is now 8:45."

"Eight forty-five. Um...yes, thanks, Monica."

He looked at the clock on his computer screen, and sure enough, he only had fifteen minutes left to setup in the boardroom. He gave the proposal a once over and had to admit it was perfectly done.

He took a long swig of his coffee, packed up his suitcase and the proposal portfolio, and headed to the boardroom. When Neil pressed the down elevator button, it immediately opened up and Amanda was inside applying lip gloss to her lips.

"Good morning, Amanda. I'm on my way down now," Neil said hastily.

Amanda exited the elevator. "Just turn on your charm and wits, and they'll love your work, Neil. We have crossed every T and dotted every I, so this should be a walk in the park."

As the doors were about to close, she stuck her hand in to stop the elevator from closing.

"Do you want to do lunch today...so you can brief me on the

meeting?"

Amanda's hopeful gaze gave Neil an ounce of discomfort, but he shrugged it off as just being his nerves.

"Sure. I'll get with you on that. Oh, and I have the specifics on your desk for a new hospital we are targeting. Go over those and start working on a plan of approach. We'll go over that at lunch, too." He looked at his watch and saw it was now 8:50. "I've got to get to this meeting. I'll bring you up to date on everything later."

Amanda immediately started thinking of ways she could turn an innocent lunch date into much more. "I know one thing I really want you to bring me up to date on...," Amanda said under her breath as she pranced toward her office.

"He's a married man. Happily, I might add," Monica spat out to her boss.

"He is for now, isn't he?" Amanda shot Monica an evil look that could not be mistaken.

It was a busy day at Naytek. Old clients were calling with technical issues. New clients were calling for details. The CEOs were on the prowl, and Neil was exhausted after doing damage control for existing clients and trying to drum up new business. Neil had just hung up the phone at 2:06 p.m. when Monica Stewart, his personal secretary, buzzed in.

"Mr. Johnston."

"Yes?"

"Don't forget your meeting with the CEO of Brown Hospital at 2:30."

"Dang. Thanks." He whizzed by her desk, then toward the elevators.

Monica entered his office, picked up the schedule she made for him that he had under a stack of papers, and taped it to his PC. "I don't know why he has me to print this schedule off everyday if he's not going to look at it."

Monica had been Neil's personal secretary for three years. She was an attractive full-figured lady who carried herself with pizzazz. Neil couldn't survive a week without her and she knew it. She rolled her eyes when she saw Amanda bouncing down the hall toward Neil's office. She respected her boss a lot, and his marriage. She wondered how he could not know that Amanda was head over heels for him.

"Good afternoon, Monica."

"Same to you, Amanda. Neil's not in his office right now. Would you like to leave him a message?"

"No. I have some documents for him to sign. I'll just leave them on his desk."

"Okay." Monica had a call come in and rushed back out to her desk.

While placing the documents on Neil's desk, Amanda looked over at his monitor and saw his schedule for the day. One thing caught her eye. *REMINDER: June 24, 2008: Two-year Anniversary: Tyler Perry play -- 7 p.m.*

Peeking out the door, she saw that Monica was busy filing her nails and talking on the phone. She knew he would be in his meeting with the Brown's executives for another hour at least, so she tip-toed back over to his PC and typed up a new schedule, this one omitting the play with his wife.

"Let's see how you enjoy your little anniversary play now, wench."

★ ★ ★

Lela spent the day shopping for the perfect outfit. She got her hair, nails, and toes done and purchased a brand new bottle of Rapture perfume. While at the beauty shop, NaQuetta told her that Terrance had been worrying her to death with trying to get her to have Lela call him. He left his number for her to give to Lela. Though Lela doubted she would ever use the number, she took it and put it in her purse.

"You're still going to watch the kids for me tonight, right?" Lela asked NaQuetta.

"I told you I would. Just bring them over here when they get out of school. I'm gonna leave early this evening," NaQuetta assured her friend.

By 5:30 p.m., Lela was dressed to impress. Her black Vera Wang chiffon silk dress, Ralph Lauren sling backs, and Jimmy Choo chain evening bag looked lovely together. She wanted everything to be perfect since she planned on talking to Neil about her going back to work over dinner.

While waiting for Neil to get home, she pressed the button on her answering machine to retrieve her voice messages. The first few messages were from Antwan and Jalan, wishing her a happy anniversary. There was also a message from Neil's boss, but the one that made her stop in her tracks was the one from Neil.

Hey, babe. Please fix me a plate so I can catch a quick bite to eat. I'll be home in thirty minutes, but I have to leave shortly after that because I have an impromptu meeting tonight.

She played the message several times trying to make sure she got it right. *"...an impromptu meeting tonight..."* Yeah, she heard it right. Twenty minutes later, she heard his car pull up.

"Have you forgotten you were taking me to the Tyler Perry play tonight?"

"Was that tonight?" He grabbed his head and massaged his temples. He had forgotten about the play.

"I did forget, sweetheart, but I'm not going to be able to make it. I promise I will make it up to you as soon as we get this mess straightened up in the office. You look good as hell, though." He kissed her on the cheek, walked past her into the kitchen, and grabbed his plate out of the microwave.

His blasé attitude was crawling all over her skin. "What do you mean 'make it up'? This is the last day the play is in town." She started pouting. "I already bought our tickets and everything. You promised to take me to the show, plus have you forgotten what today is?"

"It's June twenty fourth."

"And...?"

"Sweetheart, I'm sorry I forgot that today is our anniversary. Happy Anniversary!" Neil closed the space between them and pulled his wife into a tight embrace. "I have been so wrapped up in work that it completely slipped my mind. I know how bad you've wanted to go see this play, but I'm going to have to make it up to you."

"What could have come up so important that you have to postpone celebrating our anniversary?" Lela could not believe her ears. "I accepted the fact that you couldn't take the day off because you have this important account you are working on, but the least you could do is take me on the date you *promised* me tonight." Her face crumpled when she saw he was not going to give in. Her spirit that was glowing five minutes ago was dimming fast and tears streamed down her face.

Caught up in his own world, Neil could not comprehend the hurt and pain that something as simple as him missing a play would cause his wife, but to her, it meant so much more. She'd accepted the fact that he was never home, but now the date she'd planned so much for was another empty promise.

"I told you how important this deal is. Deals like this will have us set for life." He avoided telling her that his meeting was with

Amanda to go over some stats. He also had to proof read some documents for another client. Amanda wanted to meet at her house, but instead, he reserved a conference room at Naytek. This had to be done tonight since his flight would leave tomorrow.

"And what life is it when you're always gone and I'm always here alone with the kids? I'm sorry. I'm getting emotional. I'll manage; I always do." She walked away from him and leaped up the stairs.

Neil followed behind her. He tapped on the bathroom door and said, "I'm sorry. I'll make it up to you, sweetheart. I promise."

"I know, Neil. I'll see you after the play. Go ahead."

"Not until you come out and give me a hug."

The door opened slowly. Lela composed herself, putting on her happy face, so he could not see through to her broken spirit. Not that he would take the time to look anyway, when there was always work that needed to be done.

They hugged.

"Why don't you ask NaQuetta to go with you?" he suggested.

She forced a smile, and with all of the phony enthusiasm she could collect, she replied, "Sure." She knew NaQuetta was watching the kids for her, but she wanted him to hurry and leave. Leave her sight. Right now, she couldn't stand him at all. "I'll see you after the play, Neil."

Hearing his ignition start and his engine roar as he drove away cut Lela like a knife. She tried unsuccessfully to fight off thoughts that Neil may be leaving her to be with another woman. Amanda even crossed her mind once or twice. Then she thought, *yeah, he has another woman all right, his presentations, his clients, his business trips. That's his other woman.*

Pulling herself out of her pity, she phoned her friend Tracey and got no answer. Determined she would not fall victim to her sorrows tonight, she looked in the mirror and fixed her makeup. While reaching into her purse for her beach bronze lip gloss, she ran across Terrance's number. She walked over and stood in front of her full-length mirror, looking herself up and down. Gloating over her finished product, puffy eyes and all, she said, "I do look good. I can't believe my husband, *my husband*, just walked out on me after I did all of this for him." She felt another wave of sadness trying to overtake her, but fought it off. "No need for this night to go to waste."

She dialed Tracey's number again and got no answer. She wasn't even answering her cell phone. She called Monica, but she was stuck in Naytek working for Amanda this evening. She went back to her purse, picked up the folded piece of paper, and dialed the numbers on it.

A deep voice answered. "Hello."

"Hi, Terrance."

"Lela?" Surprise filled his voice.

With a slight smile, she answered, "Yes."

"Hey. Now this is a pleasant surprise. I see NaQuetta finally gave you my number."

"Yes. I didn't think I'd be using it, but here I am. I hope I didn't catch you at a bad time."

"Not at all. I was just sitting here about to watch a movie. Nothing really. How are you doing?"

"I've had better days, but you can make this one much better if you will go to Tyler Perry's new play with me. It starts at seven."

"What? You mean your husband doesn't have you on lock," he replied, not really caring about her husband.

Lela masked her emotions. "He's not available."

"Really? Well, he's a crazy man. I'd always be available for you."

"Sure you *say* that. Well, meet me at the front gate of the Civic Center at seven. I'll be wearing a black dress and my hair is down, so you may not recognize me."

"Oh, I'll find you. I'm jumping in the shower now."

"I'll be waiting in the lobby."

"See you soon."

Terrance was standing outside waiting for Lela when she arrived at the Civic Center. She was feeling uneasy about being out with another man, and when she saw him standing at the top of the stairway looking like Morris Chestnut's twin brother, all kinds of thoughts danced through her mind. In an attempt to relax, she took a deep breath.

"Dang, look at you, dressed all fly. You must have been sitting by the phone waiting for someone to call," Lela said, breaking the ice.

"This ain't nothing. I always dress for the occasion. How are you tonight?" he asked, rubbing near her puffy eyes.

"I've had better days, trust me."

"That brings me to my next question. To what do I owe this honor to take you out on a date? Why aren't you with your husband tonight?"

"Because my husband has a date with work, as usual. Let's not talk about it. The show is about to start."

Looping his arm in Lela's, he escorted her into the show. He hoped if he played his cards right tonight, it would not be the last night he would get to spend with Lela. Looking at her sexy dress, and knowing how loving and caring Lela was, he wondered how any man could choose work over her anyway.

The show was funny, spiritual and heartwarming, and dinner was even cozier. Lela had to catch herself from getting caught up in Terrance's charm.

"Thanks for meeting me, Terrance. I really had a good time."

"Anytime. All you have to do is call me when you need someone to talk to."

"I may do that."

Terrance's quick peck on her cheek ended their outing. Or was it a date? *Naaah!* Lela thought, *just spending time with a friend because my husband's not available. Okay, sounds like a date, but naaah!*

When Lela woke up the next morning, Neil was not in bed. His luggage was by the front door, so she knew he had not left yet. She remembered his flight was leaving at 3 p.m., and she had to take him to the airport at eleven o'clock this morning.

She got up and dressed the kids and herself. After taking the kids to school and daycare and returning home, she found Neil in his office on the computer.

When he saw her walk in, his eyes lit up. "Hey, babe." He regretted letting her spend their anniversary alone, especially since the information Amanda had to show him, which she claimed was *so* important, was nothing more than some papers she printed off the internet and something he could have located himself. He started to wonder about Amanda. He allowed her to waste his time, when he could have spent an unforgettable evening celebrating his marriage.

Visions of Lela's curves in that silky chiffon dress with her curly, shoulder-length hair sent regret all through him.

"Neil." She was still upset about him dismissing their date last night, and could not hide it in the sound of her voice. "We need to be leaving to get you to the airport on time."

"We don't have to leave until one o'clock, so I have three hours. Look, I'm sorry about..."

She held her hand up. "Save it. I don't want to hear it. You did what was important to you, and that's all that matters, right?" She smiled contemptuously. "Just know I enjoyed the show."

"I'm sorry. I should not have put work ahead of us. I will never do that again."

"Neil, you have put work ahead of us from day one and I have never complained, but I'm tired. I knew when I married you that you were married to your work already and I was your second wife, so I never ever hassled you about it."

She felt the tears welling up in her eyes, but forced herself to gain composure.

"All I asked for was one night with you before you left, and you couldn't give me that. That one night is gone, never to come again, so we don't have anything to talk about today."

She turned to walk toward the bedroom. Neil caught her arm before she could make it to the hallway.

"Lela, I was wrong, *so wrong*. I'm begging you; please don't let this be the way I leave you. I can't stand the thought of going out of town with you this upset with me. If something happened to you while I was gone, I could not live with myself knowing I left you hurt. I'm sorry."

He pushed her chin up with his finger and kissed her lips.

No matter how bad he hurt her by walking out on her on their anniversary, she could not deny the feeling in her heart. She kissed him back, and said, "Apology accepted. Now, let's get you ready to go."

30
Royal Rumble

Neil was back home and preparing to travel with Amanda, yet again, to help her close the Richardson Norcross deal. Even though Richardson Norcross was supposed to be Amanda's baby, she convinced Christian that she needed Neil to tag along.

Lela was not looking forward to being alone for a week without her husband, so she moped around the house. Since she knew Neil would spend the next two days getting prepared for the trip, she decided to do something constructive with her time...go shopping.

She called Tonya early at seven in the morning.

"Hello," Tonya answered, sounding sleepy.

"Hey, girl. You want to go shopping or hang out today?"

"Shopping? You don't have to ask me twice. Is it on you?"

"You know me better than that. I guess I'll expect you in about three hours."

"Yeah, I should be there at least by noon."

"Okay. Drive safe, sis."

By that evening, Tonya and Lela had literally 'shopped until they dropped'. Unlike her old frugal self, Lela charged up over two grand worth of clothes, shoes, and other household knickknacks. They were walking out of Neiman Marcus when Lela spotted Amanda approaching.

Amanda looked like a runway model in her form fitting shirt dress. Her walk exuded confidence, and her whole disposition crawled Lela's skin.

"Damn white girls. Ain't nothing sacred. We can't even have *our* men," Lela turned and said to Tonya out of the blue.

"Girl, what are you talking about?" Tonya was confused. She continued looking at the price tag of a chiffon top she had been eyeing in the Colonial Mall for a couple of weeks now.

"Look to your right. The chick with the pink dress, coming our way," Lela said under her breath.

"I see," Tonya replied.

"Hey, Lela. How are you?" Amanda said cheerfully.

"I'm doing good. How about yourself?" Lela asked, exerting the same phony enthusiasm.

"Good. Where's that husband of yours? No, don't tell me. He's probably working. He never takes any time off. I keep telling him that wrinkles are going to take over that handsome face of his if he keeps on working so much," Amanda said with a smile that had a hint of suggestion. "You know *we* wouldn't want our guy to lose his glow."

"Yes, he's at work now. He will be *home* soon. I take good care of him at *home*, so you don't have to worry about him losing anything. I'm the reason he's *glowing* any way."

"I'm sure you do take good care of him. I know *I* do when he's in the office all those long nights. Don't slip Lela. There is *always* someone waiting in the wind."

Lela's head was pounding. First, she walks in the office to find this woman hugged up on her husband, and now, she's throwing insinuations around. That's not even to mention a few nights ago when Amanda called *her* house expecting *her* husband to come over and escort her into her apartment because she was too scared to go in alone. There is a thin line between getting a pass and a beat down.

"No, she didn't." She looked at Tonya, who already knew what was up.

Tonya grabbed her arm and tried to calm her. "Girl, chill, damn. You don't have anything to worry about. You're his wife, not her. Neil ain't going nowhere, especially nowhere with her."

Lela came back to her senses and backed down, picking her shopping bags up off the floor. "You're right. I don't know why I let her get under my skin like that."

The beef was temporarily squashed until Amanda spoke up, mimicking Ebonics at Lela. She had the nerve to be rolling her eyes and popping her neck with it, too.

"Oh, you gone let yo' friend talk you down Shanaynay? I thought you were Neil's gangster boo or sumtin'? Go on and show me wutz crackin'. Do you. Jus don't be surprised when you find out Amanda ain't yo average white girl. Try me."

In a blind rage, Lela rushed Amanda and started swinging. The security guard, who had been watching the entire exchange, caught her arm before she landed a blow.

Amanda laughed as she walked off. Before leaving, though, she said one last thing. "See, that's why Neil needs a real woman. Look at your pathetic self."

By that time, another security guard was approaching them while talking into his walkie talkie. Tonya noticed him first, but who wouldn't? He had silky hair like he was rocking a wave kit and skin made of brown sugar, but he was all male. His prominent chest protruded through his button-up blue shirt, and she had never seen any man wear blue khakis like he did.

"Ladies, is there a problem?" He motioned to the first security guard on the scene that he would handle it.

Tonya couldn't speak. Lela sensed her friend was having one of her mental block moments, so she spoke for them.

"No. No problem. We were just leaving." She could not believe that here she was about to scrap and Tonya was trying to make a love connection. Lela wanted to catch up with Amanda in the parking lot.

"Good, because I hate to have to escort two beautiful ladies like you out of the mall like criminals. You have more class than that, and here you are about to tear into that lady. I would hate to have to hold you for the cops." Making eye contact with Tonya, the security guard added, "Have a good day, ladies. Maybe we'll bump into each other again, but not under these circumstances."

"Maybe," Tonya murmured, blushing like a schoolgirl. Just as he turned to walk away, she stopped him. "Hey, I didn't get your name."

He pointed to his name badge. "Andre, and you?"

"I'll be at the car," Lela said. "Good looking out, Tonya."

She flipped her cell phone open to call Neil. If she knew anything about Amanda, she knew she probably had already called to report the incident to him. *Damn. I wish I would have just started wailing on her ass as soon as she stepped to me.*

In the parking lot, Lela stood by Tonya's car talking on her cell phone. Amanda was nowhere in sight. She snapped her phone closed when she saw Tonya approaching.

"You know that…woman has already called Neil and told him that I tried to jump on her. I wish I could get my hands on her."

Tonya placed her bags in the trunk and got into the driver seat. "She did what?"

"Called and told on me. Told Neil I tried to jump on her because she asked how he was doing." Lela put her arm on Tonya's shoulder and said, "On the real, as cozy as those two are, I wonder sometimes.

"Last night Amanda called waking us out of our sleep. Apparently, when she got home all of the lights were out in her apartment and she was too afraid to go in. Of course, she could not get in contact with any of her family and thought Neil would be her night in shining armor. She expected him to come over there and escort her into her apartment in the middle of the night."

"That girl's got issues."

"You should have seen her face when I rolled down my window and said 'hi Amanda.' She had a deflated look that only a woman could recognize. The woman is after my man, but I can't get him to see it. I better not ever find out Neil has been with Amanda."

"I told you that's the least of your worries. I have a sixth sense about these things, and I just don't think Neil is creeping with Amanda. She may want it, and want it badly enough to mess with your head every chance she gets, but she's just acting out of desperation more than anything."

"You had a sixth sense about me having a girl and I had Jalan, so…"

"Well that was different. I know I'm right about Neil and Miss Amanda." Tonya changed the subject filling Lela in about her date with Mr. Brown Sugar Security. They then tried to enjoy the rest of their shopping trip.

The ladies worked up an appetite fussing with Amanda. Tonya wanted some fish, so she pulled into the drive-thru window at Captain D's. This had been their spot since they were in high school. When they were sixteen, the very first day Lela got to drive her car without her parents, she picked Tonya up and they ended up in Captain D's with the munchies.

When Tonya pulled up to the window, the cashier immediately took their order.

"Welcome to Capem Dee's, may I take yo orda?" she asked while popping her gum into the intercom.

Tonya placed their usual orders and pulled around to the window. Just as she was about to ask the sistah to add some extra tarter sauce with her order, a prissy-looking white girl with Jamie on her nametag stood at the window. Tonya didn't think much of it. It is not unusual that one person takes orders and another collects the money. Then Jamie spoke, and what looked like a platinum grill reflected off the window.

"Datta be six seminy two. You want taada with dat?" Tonya looked at Lela, who was already about to burst a blood vessel trying not to laugh. Tonya handed the girl the money, and she repeated, "You want taada with dat?"

"What did she say?" Tonya mouthed to Lela.

"Tarter sauce, girl. Taada," Lela added, putting extra emphasis on the A like Jamie.

The girl looked like she could have been Bill Gates' daughter, until she opened her mouth. She talked and acted worse than Wanda from In Living Color. Tonya snuck in a few chuckles while the girl counted her change back.

"Yeah, we want some of *dat taada*," Tonya answered.

"Aiight den," the girl replied, not even realizing she was being mocked.

After the girl handed them their orders, Tonya did her spot check to make sure the order was correct and then drove off.

Lela was first to weigh in. "See, girl, we laughing, but these white girls got a plan. To attract *our* men. They speak Ebonics for the thugs and flip to the educated mode for the black businessmen." Lela spoke as though she had it all figured out.

"Whatever. If a man chooses to roll with that there working at Capem Dee's," Tonya teased, "...and speaking Ebonics to boot, then they deserve each other. No sweat off my back. I don't want no black, white, or brown man who has been messing around with a broad like that. He wouldn't be able to handle the game how I lay it down anyway. To the left with that."

"True, true." Lela got silent and looked out of the window, something she did whenever she was in deep thought. She realized it was not white women she had the problem with, just Amanda Broady.

Tonya picked up on her change in mood.

"What is it?"

"What? What?" Lela wished her friend didn't know her so well.

"See, you only repeat yourself when you are worried about something."

"It's just that Neil has been spending so much time on this Richardson Norcross project with Amanda. If it's not the Richardson Norcross project, then it's another one. Our relationship is being tested in the worst way. Now, they are going to be gone together for a week in Chicago." She paused. "It's not even that he's working on the project with her. It's the vibe I get from her whenever I come around Neil and her. She makes me feel like I'm the one intruding on them."

"But you can't intrude on what is yours, babe. Amanda tries to make you feel that way to intimidate you. Trust, if Neil was giving her any kind of play, that grimy hoe would have let you know by now. She would relish in having a taste of what's yours. I don't think she could keep it a secret."

"She's been trying to make me feel like she's got the upper hand since Neil spends more hours in the office *with her* than he does at home. The other night, I stopped by with the kids, and she was practically sitting in his lap, rolling up his sleeves for him."

"Sitting in his lap? What the…"

"He jumped up all scared looking, and explained how he had to change out of his business shirt into a t-shirt from his gym bag because she had spilled coffee on it. I know he likes his sleeves rolled up on his t–shirts, but the sight of her touching my man's arms about drove me to the brink, girl. I was about to bust a cap up in his Fortune 500 Company." Lela went from sad to fuming. "A man can only be so strong when he is not getting, or should I say giving, any at home, and then is always in the company of another woman."

"Why are you just telling me about this little incident? What did you do?" Tonya already pictured in her mind Lela letting them have it.

"Nothing. I couldn't hear or see anything but red. It was little Jalan's babbling that rattled some sense into me. Then, when I saw the smirk on Amanda's face, it spoke multitudes. Too bad Neil can't catch on to her antics, or maybe he has and is just playing dumb for my benefit. I have been through too much, and I couldn't handle being hurt again.

"You just don't understand, Tonya. Neil is in my system, and I *used* to be in his. When he is not working, he is good to me in all the ways a woman wants a man to be."

Tonya said, "I know, girl." Lela's saga was opening up wounds from her own love life.

"But you don't know the half. I know Neil has a big appetite, but he hasn't touched me since I went to his office two weeks ago."

"In the office, huh? I'm sure Amanda was spinning in her heels."

"Yeah, I think we gave Naytek employees an earful." Lela

giggled recounting that day.

"But like I was saying, when he comes home, it's after nine...eight if I'm lucky...and he is too zonked out to even have a ten-minute conversation with me, let alone sex me.

"Just knowing he's holed up in his cozy office that he blew my back out in more times than one with Amanda makes me nervous. Then with him not desiring me, it only makes it all the worse."

"Lela, I understand your pain, but there are two sides to every story, so don't rush to a conclusion on this. Neil is probably just worn down from work. You said it yourself he has been working hard. He worships the ground you walk on. You need to sit him down and have a heart to heart. Let him know how you feel about everything that is going on. He should understand why this makes you insecure. Maybe you can convince him to take a few days off after he comes back from Chicago."

"Maybe."

Lela and Tonya went to the park to eat their lunch, both mulling over their own relationship issues.

After hearing Lela's concerns, Neil promised he would put Amanda in her place and make more time for home. He also suggested that they start attending church on Sundays. He felt a lot of Lela's insecurities stemmed from the fact that they were not rooted in the church. Not knowing what else he could say to convince his wife that he was totally committed to her, he thought of the only other thing that could persuade her, God.

That Sunday, they attended Higher Peace Missionary Baptist Church, where ironically the sermon topic was infidelity. The preacher specifically spoke about 'the snake in the grass.' Neil had never accused Lela of cheating, although she had ample opportunity given that he was always away on business and she was a stay-at-home mom. There was plenty of motive and opportunities for her to cheat, but his mind was not programmed that way. Hands down, he was faithful. He had loyalty to her and trusted in his heart that she felt the same for him. He knew he had a good woman and didn't question that.

Lela, on the other hand, was always on him about what he did while he was on business trips, what he did at work, and wanting to know if women tried to hit on him. Of course, women approached him. He was fine, successful, and had a personality a woman could fall in love with.

He had women dropping anything from subtle hints to downright booty calls when he was out of town. Ninety percent of the people in the medical transcription industry were women, so being hit on came with the territory. Most of those offers ended up in a conversation about Lela, which turned out to be quite the mistress deterrent.

He thought back long and hard to when his wife became insecure in their relationship. For sure this was a quality he would have picked up on before he married her. Mulling it over, he realized she had always been that way, and Amanda had been the main ingredient of Lela's distrust.

Amanda was a beautiful woman in her own right, from her brown-tanned skin to her curly blond hair. For Neil, she could have been Beyoncé Knowles. She still was not getting any play from him. Lela was the only person with the key to his heart.

Neil bowed his head and prayed for his marriage.

After church, they chose to go to Anthony's Restaurant and actually dined out for a change. This was a well overdue family outing. Antwan and Jalan giggled, played, and enjoyed being out with their father.

"Daddy, I want some spaghetti." Antwan beamed.

"Dayee, sketti." Jalan broke his crayon in two as he colored wildly on his kiddy menu.

"You guys sure that's going to fill you up?"

"Yes, sir," Antwan answered for the both of them.

"Well, spaghetti it is." Then to Lela, he said, "They're ordering like little men."

"Yes, Neil, that's what I have been trying to tell you. They are growing fast."

Neil dropped his head down to his menu. Most successful businesspeople had to make sacrifices, and family was usually the sacrificial lamb. He had some self-evaluation to do, because he did not want to turn around and be attending Jalan's high school graduation and never have gotten the chance to throw the football with him on Saturdays or be a little league dad.

They proceeded to enjoy a delicious dinner mixed with conversation and laughter.

31
On the Road Again

"**D**id you pack your ties?" Lela asked as she hurried around the house tying up loose ends for Neil's Chicago trip.

"Yes, baby."

"Did you put your suits in the trunk yet?"

"Yes, baby."

"Did you get your presentation CD out of the computer?"

"No. I almost forgot that, and it's the most important thing. What would I do without you? "

"I'll never let you find out. Now don't forget the thing that is really the most important." Lela puckered her lips for a kiss.

"You know I can't forget that." He gave her a long, passionate kiss while giving her his trademark rub up and down her back.

"Neil," Lela whispered in his ear, "don't go starting something you can't finish. You know you have to get going."

"I have a few minutes before my plane leaves, and we pretty much have everything together, so can a brother get fifteen minutes with his wife?"

"Hell, after the three hours you just got with me, I don't think so. You couldn't be a minute-man if you tried."

"Let's try it and see."

Looking down, she said, "Hmmm. Let me check and see if I have any medicine left for all that swelling. It's really huge."

Unbeknownst to the two of them, Antwan and Jalan stood there enjoying the show, mouths wide open.

"Mommy, Daddy can use my medicine," Antwan said, concerned about his father.

Lela put her hands over her mouth and looked at Neil, then back at Antwan.

"Antwan! How long have you two been standing there?"

"Never mind that. You two want to finish up your puzzles while I finish talking to Mommy about my trip?"

Jalan nodded his head. On the way down to the recreation room, Antwan asked his father, "Is your finger alright?"

"Yes. Mommy is going to put something on it."

"Antwan," Neil said, rubbing his son's head, "keep an eye on your little brother while your mom and I go over the details of my trip. Then I'll be down to play Sonic with you in a few minutes."

"Sure, Dad."

"Better yet, let me call and see if Carol will watch you two while we talk. It may take a while."

Neil made a call to their neighbor, who had children close to Jalan and Antwan's age, and asked if she could keep an eye on them for an hour.

"Sure thing," Carol gladly agreed.

Neil helped Jalan into his shoes and watched his sons until they were safely in Carol's house. When he made it upstairs, Lela was in their bedroom making up the bed, wearing nothing but a lacy bra and garter skirt minus the panties.

Leaning up against the doorsill, he took a minute to enjoy the view before making his presence known. His attempt to be quiet failed when a light moan slipped through his lips.

"No need to make this up just yet." He pulled the covers back and got in the bed, pulling her in with him. Pulling on the slinky skirt, he asked, "When did you get this?"

"You like?" Lela laughed. "Just a little sumtin sumtin I picked up for you yesterday."

"Well, since it's for me, model it for me, *please*. Let me see what it do. I want the full treatment, too."

He drank in her every move as she sashayed to the middle of their room. She turned on "It Seems Like You're Ready" by R. Kelly and performed for him like stripping was her profession. She moved her body to the beat, and it wasn't long before he grabbed and devoured her body.

Before they knew anything, they had been at it for an hour.

"See, I told you that you were no minute-man."

Totally spent, Neil contemplated blowing the trip, taking the kids to Lela's mother for the night, and holding her hostage in their bedroom for the next week. But as usual, duty called. He showered, then went and got Jalan and Antwan from next door.

"Thanks, Carol." Carol was dressed provocatively in a halter and tight hip hugger jeans, which was out of character for her. Even though she was pushing fifty, her body was tight and fit, but she normally played the Mary Poppins role. Neil thought her one-hour transformation was ironic. "You look nice, Carol."

"Thank you, Neil," she replied in a low, sexy voice. "And I'm always here for *you*. If there is anything, *any-thing*, I can do for you, you know where to find me."

"Okay." Gathering up Jalan and Antwan, he rushed home and beat them both in a game of Sonic.

Pulling into the airport drop-off, Lela wished him luck with his client. He quickly retrieved his bags from the trunk, and Lela watched him scurry into the building.

"Alright, my little guy and big guy, what do you want to do today?" Lela asked. When Neil was away, Antwan was the man of the house, but Jalan, who was only one, was just as protective of Lela.

"Skating...," was Antwan's first choice. "Can-dee...," was Jalan's.

"How about we pick up some candy at the skating rink?"

"Yeah!" they both cheered.

Lela admired her two men, just as she admired Neil.

Neil left Sunday, and by Wednesday, Lela was lonely. At least when he was at home she could depend on having a warm body in bed next to her at night. She had done everything she could think of to wind down, but still could not relax enough to sleep.

At midnight, without even a chance of sleep happening any time soon, Lela hoped hearing Neil's voice would calm her enough to sleep.

Earlier, he brought her up to speed on how business was going for him in Chicago. In the three days there, he had covered a lot of ground with Richardson Norcross. He was convinced the vice president over health information technology was ready to sign on the bottom line once all of the kinks were worked out to suit their way of doing business. That was at 9 p.m., and he was so tired he told her he was going to turn in early. She hated to wake him up, but at that moment, she needed him.

She dialed his room, and when the line picked up, she heard laughter. No talking, just laughter. Then she heard a woman's voice. She thought she must have dialed the wrong number, so she hung up and dialed his room again.

This time, Neil answered. "Hello."

The same laughter was in the background. The same woman's voice. Amanda.

"Neil? I just tried calling you and hung up because I thought I had the wrong room."

"That was you? I wondered who was calling and hanging up."

She thought, *A woman in your room in the middle of the night, and you have questions?*

She gave him the benefit of the doubt, and answered, "I thought surely I had the wrong number because of all of the noise. What's going on there?"

At that moment, the female, whose voice she recognized to be Amanda's, let out another bout of irritating laughter.

"Neil, you are too funny. You're next."

The shriek of Amanda's voice made Lela see a red haze. Her voice choked up.

"I know that's not Amanda?" She could feel her heart gaining weight as she waited for his answer. "What is she doing in *your* room this late?"

"Yeah, it is," he said, motioning for his company to quiet down. "We took the client out tonight. We all had a few drinks, so I thought it would be best that we went over our closing strategy since we didn't get to do that earlier this evening. Mark is here, also, and Trey just stepped out to get some ice."

At that moment, Trey must have stepped back into the room because she heard Neil say, "It's your cousin, Lela."

"Tell cuzzo I said hi," Trey said from in the background.

Eager to ease the tension, Neil relayed the message. "Trey says hello."

"Oh really?"

"Hold on, baby."

She could hear him tell the crew that they would meet in the morning and that he was going to call it a night.

Once the room was cleared, he positioned himself on his pillow. He knew he had some explaining to do.

"I'm glad you called, Lela. I miss you."

"I bet you do. Looks like you got plenty company," she said

viciously, her tone more cutting than her words.

Instantly, he lost all the buzz he had gotten from the mixed drinks they had at the restaurant. Knowing what the problem was, Neil skipped the pleasantries and went straight to the gut of what was bothering his wife.

"First of all, you know Amanda has her own room. I deal with her the same way I deal with Mark, Trey, and the rest of my associates. Mark, Trey, Amanda, and I were *all* in my room. Even though we are away on business, I try to keep it fun as much as possible. We all work better when we're not stressed."

Neil laid his head back on his pillow. He didn't want his wife to be upset with him. In his mind, she had nothing to worry about as far as Amanda was concerned.

"You know I don't trust that woman."

"But you do trust me, right? So you don't have anything to worry about. She works with me and that's it. There is no competition."

Hearing the seriousness in his voice, she digressed, "Okay, but she still doesn't need to be in your room with you alone."

"You're right, but Mark was here, and Trey only stepped out for a second. It won't happen again." Neil was getting tired of having to explain himself. He looked over at Lela's picture sitting on his nightstand and imagined what she looked like when she was mad.

"I'm only feeling one particular woman who owns a garter skirt and a lacy bra and knows how to give a great going away party. I'm still in a tailspin from that. How can I think about another woman?"

Lela was melting and he could tell.

"Besides, you're here with me always."

"What do you mean by that?"

"I take your picture with me every time I go out of town." He leaned over and kissed the picture. "I'm kissing you goodnight now."

"I'm blowing you a kiss, too, but right now, I need so much more than a kiss. I need you here."

"Me, too, babe." Neil yawned. "I'll call you tomorrow afternoon. And Lela?"

"Yes." She still had a tad of attitude in her voice.

"Stop acting jealous. You know that really bothers me. I told you I'm not feeling her like that."

"Keep her out of your room then. You know how she treats me and talks to me. The next time I see her, she'll probably be bragging about how much fun she had in your suite."

"Done. I wasn't thinking. We'll meet in the lobby or schedule time in a conference room from now on. But you...you stop tripping, woman. You are my one and only, so act like it." Wiping the wrinkles from the frown off his forehead, he took a deep breath and said, "I love you."

"I love you, too. Good luck on your presentation tomorrow."

Lela was having trouble sleeping when she called Neil, but now, she really couldn't sleep. Thoughts of Amanda flaunting around in Neil's hotel room had her tossing and turning in the bed.

The nerve of her to be up in my man's room giggling all over the place. She gets on my last nerve! I need to call Trey and see if I can get the 411 on what's going on during these trips.

* * *

Amanda was pissed to high hell that Lela called Neil. *Why does she always have to call and mess up everything? I'm getting tired of her! I'm going to have to get rid of her...and for good. I just have to wait until the time is right, but oh little Mrs. Lela, you will have your day to squirm.* Amanda laughed at her devilish thoughts.

She almost had some time alone with Neil in his hotel room tonight, but Lela's call shook him up, and took him all out of the mood Amanda had tried so hard to set. The two Absolute and cranberry drinks she had coaxed him into drinking in order to wind down had taken his professionalism down a few notches. Amanda had been working on him all day, softening him up so she could move in for the kill. Her plan was to seduce the hell out of him, too.

She took a long cool shower and then put on the red lingerie set that she purchased just for Neil. Pulling out his picture she had cut from the company newsletter, she placed it on her pillow. She imagined lying in his arms as they lay together in her bed.

We belong together, she thought. She looked into his eyes in the picture until she drifted off to sleep.

32
Home Sweet Home

N eil smiled when he saw the extravagant Pointe Shores sign at the entrance of his neighborhood from the window of the taxicab. This was his first time coming home from a business trip early. It was twelve o'clock midnight and he could not wait to surprise Lela. *I can't wait to get home to my baby.*

He had been working so hard on closing Richardson Norcross; he was ready for some much needed time off. He had been successful in getting Richardson Norcross to sign on the dotted line early; hence, he was on the first thing smoking from Chicago and getting ready to be at his home within seconds.

Fifty thousand dollar bonus check for closing this deal. He calculated his earnings and boasted to himself. To celebrate, he purchased Lela an eight-carat diamond-cut bracelet at a well-known jeweler in Chi-town.

Lela is not going to believe it. He smiled as he thought about the good news he had to share with his wife.

He was proud to have her in his corner, supportive of his career and helping him to achieve new heights during their marriage. She had prepared presentations, mailed gifts to his clients, and gave him the support he needed to feel invincible.

When the cab pulled in front of the house, he paid the cab and went in through the garage. His most obvious observation was that Lela's car was missing.

"That's strange. Maybe she let NaQuetta use her car," he mumbled to himself. He knew NaQuetta's car had been giving her trouble, and it was not out of character for Lela to let her use her car from time to time.

Inside the house, Neil stopped into Jalan's room first and noticed he was not there. The same thing in Antwan's room. He went into the master bedroom and the same thing, empty.

Sometimes Lela would spend the night at her mother's when he was out of town because she was scared to be in the house alone, but usually, she would tell him where she was going to be. He dialed Miss Rachel's number.

"Hello," Miss Rachel answered groggily.

"Hey, Momma Rachel. Sorry to call you so late, but can I speak to my wife?"

"Oh, hey, Neil. How are you enjoying Chicago?"

"Just fine. It was work. I'm home now and looking for my wife and kids."

"She's not here. She stayed at NaQuetta's tonight. She's been over there all day helping her pack. That NaQuetta's moving again. I don't know why that girl can't just get in one place and stay." Rachel managed to hold a conversation through her sleepy haze. "Oh, but the boys are here."

"Okay. I'll try to catch her there. Sorry to wake you."

He hung up the phone a bit confused. He talked to Lela earlier that day and she didn't mention anything about helping NaQuetta pack.

When NaQuetta opened her door at 12:30 a.m., she asked Neil, "What are you doing here so late at night?"

"I came to see my lovely lady." When he noticed the shock on NaQuetta's face, he clarified, "Lela. Can you go get her?"

"Oh…uh. Hold on."   She stood there looking like a deer caught in headlights before she finally spat out, "She's not here." She had to tell the truth. Neil would push his way in the door if she said Lela was in the house but could not produce her.

"Well, wasn't she here helping you pack? Her mother said she was here with you. Hold on," he said as he dialed Lela's mother's house again. Her mother told him that Lela had not come back there.

Next, he dialed Lela's cell phone. He was in a mix between worried and furious.

Lela's cell phone rang, waking her from a deep slumber.

"Hello," she murmured, sounding as if she had just been wakened from a satisfying sleep.

Her husband picked up on it immediately. "Woman!" He was

now past furious. He was cocked and loaded. "Where are you?" He paced back and forth on NaQuetta's porch.

Lela was now erect on her feet, wide awake.

"I'm at NaQuetta's house. I fell asleep helping her pack. You know she is mov..."

"Don't give me that bull!" He shook his head back and forth. "I'm standing in front of NaQuetta's house right now, so come on out then if you're up in there."

He paused, waiting for an answer, and when she did not respond, he continued. "I know you're not here because I'm here looking for you in the middle of the night, and NaQuetta says you are not here.

Insecurities Neil didn't know were possible for him to have surfaced. He knew of other men in the office who had affairs while on business but he had always been faithful to Lela, believing that if he did, what goes around would come around.

Yet, here he stood on NaQuetta's doorstep in the middle of the night being deceived by his wife. *Lela, don't do this to us.* He held out hope that everything was on the cool.

Lela dropped the phone to the floor and tried to collect herself. Her heart was beating so fast, she could hear it and see it beating through her lace gown. Neil's routine was like clockwork. He always called when he was on his way home and had never come home in the middle of the night.

"Oh my God, he's home!" She knew she had to talk to him, so she picked the phone back up, placing it to her ear.

"Lela?" Neil called out to her, still holding out hope that there would be an innocent explanation for his wife's midnight escapade.

"Yes, baby," she whimpered.

"Is everything okay, Lela?" Terrance said as he stirred from his sleep. He did not know what was going on, but seeing Lela in this state concerned him.

Hearing the deep male's voice was all it took for Neil. His worst nightmare had come true. He was about to lose control, so he used his only strand of hope to fire off his next set of questions.

"Lela, where are you? I came home early to surprise you. The deal is closed and I bought you a gift to let you know how much I appreciate you being by my side. Now, tell me who is with you?" He knew for sure it was innocent. *It has to be*, he reassured himself over and over. *She wouldn't cheat. We are happy. Not Lela. God, not Lela!*

When she didn't answer in what he thought was sufficient time for an honest response, he lost it and started demanding answers.

"Say something, now!"

"It's not what you think."

"What am I supposed to think?"

He didn't give her time to answer. Instead, he told her what he wanted to hear. "Tell me my woman is not laid up with the next man. Huh? Tell me that. Tell me I'm not out here working every hour of the day busting my ass for my family and staying true to you and you're out running around in the middle of the night doing God knows what. Tell me that.

"You really had me worried about you. But you're all right where you are, aren't you, baby girl? Got my kids all the way in Opelika at your mother's house on a school night. And for what? So you can be free to frolic. What kind of a mother does that? Huh? Tell me that. Tell me this is not going down the way it looks. Tell me!"

Lela's cries only intensified Neil's anger.

"I just went out and spent four thousand dollars, *four thousand dollars*, on a bracelet for you. Got right on the road to come home *to you*, to talk to *you*, to make love *to you*. Guess dude done all ready took care of that for me, though, huh? Tell me this is not happening. Just tell me, Lela."

Still halfway sleep, Terrance tried to find out what was going on. When his eyes focused and he saw Lela on the phone crying, he realized exactly the cause of her distress. A screaming male's voice that he knew was Neil's blared through the phone, making it clear that her husband was aware of Lela's late night excursion. His heart felt the pain that was in Lela's eyes as she struggled to explain herself to her husband. He stroked her shoulder silently in an attempt to ease her pain. He felt responsible for the trouble that lay ahead of her at home.

"It's not what you think it is. I was invited to dinner by an old friend, and I must have fallen asleep."

"Who is this friend?"

"Terrance, an old friend from college. I know what it looks like, but..."

"It looks like you're not the woman I thought you were."

She sniffled. "But nothing happened."

"That's the standard response given the situation."

Lela knew she was in for the longest night ever. Even though her relationship with Terrance was not physical, in her heart of hearts, she knew what she was doing was cheating. At the moment, she could not figure out how she had gotten herself in this situation.

"Unfuckingbelievable," Neil said, looking and sounding like a broken man. "Now Lela, I'm going to ask you one more time. Where are you?"

The way he talked to her made her feel like the scum of the earth. She had never heard him curse and talk so harshly to her. She felt she would be better off explaining things to him face to face. "Cornelius, I'm... I'm on my way home. I'll talk to you when I get there."

"You do that," he replied, his voice dry and thick. He rubbed his temples, wishing he could push the rewind button and come home to find his wife lying in bed waiting for him.

Lela could hear the anger mixed with hurt in his voice, causing a pang in her heart she had never felt before. She could only think of one thing to say.

"I love you, baby."

Neil let out a long sigh. It was *love* that was causing this to hurt so much, so love was the last thing he wanted to discuss.

"I hope you got something worth hearing, because this situation is real messed up. If you can't explain you being out in the middle of the night with another man, don't come home, because no wife of mine will be out whoring around."

Lela pressed the END button on her cell phone and quickly dressed, paying close attention to details. She did not want to look like she just rolled out of the bed with a man. She made sure her hair was combed and her clothes were adjusted correctly.

She was almost out the door, when Terrance came out of the bathroom and hugged her waist from behind. His breath was hot on her neck. "What's going on, Lela? Talk to me."

She closed her eyes because she really did not need this right now. Neil was her number one priority. She turned to face Terrance.

He pulled her even closer to him, savoring what he knew could be their last intimate moment.

"When I told you I loved you, I meant every word. You're in here." He caressed his shirt above his heart.

"I have to go. Tonight was what it was. There can be no more us," Lela said, thirty seconds past ready to end this encounter. Then, she ran down the situation. "Neil is home. He has never come home early without letting me know ahead of time. That is how I have been able to spend so much time with you. Now, I'm busted and it does not feel good. I love my husband, and I cannot believe I betrayed him. Now, I have a lot of explaining to do."

"You don't have to explain anything to him," Terrance said, trying to convince her to stay. "I told you, you are welcome to stay here with me. You don't have to go anywhere." He pulled her back to the bed to sit on his lap.

"Terrance, we have gone through this before," she said, now sobbing out of control. "It's not just me I have to worry about." She thought about what she was saying and untangled herself from his grasp. "Plus, I *do* love my husband."

"Then why are you here?" He pulled her back into his arms and kissed her. This time, she did not resist. He wanted her to remember the countless lonely nights she'd spent alone when her husband left her to her own devices.

"I have to go. Let's end this here. *Please.*" Her voice trembled. "Sorry."

As she closed the door, he solemnly said, "I love you, Lela. Always have. Always will."

Lela let the door slam behind her as she rushed to her car. The ride to and from Opelika was long, but she picked up the kids from her mother's, hoping having them when she saw Neil would lighten his mood. When she got home five hours later, Neil was sitting on their bed in the dark.

She walked over to him and touched his arm while still holding Jalan in her other arm.

Without acknowledging her, he took Jalan out of her arm, took him to his room, and put him to bed. She had never seen him this way, and she vowed then and there that if she could ever make things right with him, she would not do anything to bring this side of him out again.

She went and tucked Antwan into his bed. When she looked down at her son, the gravity of the situation came alive. She thought about the fact that her kids were being shuffled around in the middle of the night because she was out spending time with another man. Guilt overtook her all at once. Her family could fall apart all in one night because of her.

Feeling sick to the stomach, she rushed to the bathroom, fearing she would throw up at any moment. Before she could lock the door, Neil pushed it open and entered the bathroom behind her. He yanked her up from her position over the toilet and was all up in her face.

He looked into her eyes, trying to find any shred of purity he could hold onto. He wanted to see the woman he fell in love with. He wanted to see the woman he was still in love with. He wanted to see the mother of his children and the woman he gave his life to, but his eyes and heart betrayed him. He could not feel anything for her but disgust at that moment.

Breaking the hardened silence, he asked, "What the hell is going on? And don't try to sugar coat it. Give it to me straight. I'ma man about mine."

Lela collected her senses. "I….I…I love you," she stuttered. She was about to give him the long story of how she met Terrance, how Terrance would call to check up on her when he was away, and how one thing led to another and she ended up at his house tonight, but she knew he would not understand. Most importantly, she wanted him to know that she had not been sexually involved with Terrance.

"You, you, you love me. Is that all I get? Neil, I've been cheating on you, but I love you," he mocked. "My kids are at your mother's house while you're MIA, lying about being at NaQuetta's, and now you can't even look at me with a straight face and tell me where you were and I…I…I love you is all you have to offer?"

He walked out of the bathroom with Lela on his heels.

"Wait, baby."

"When I called earlier, you told me you were at home, which turns out to be another one of your tangled web of lies. I didn't know we had gotten to this point. You don't know how high of a pedestal I had you on. Boy, how the mighty fall!"

Crying was all she could do. The truth was written all over her face, and he could read her like a book. She knew the truth out of her mouth would only make things worse with him being so upset, and she couldn't fix her lips to tell him that she fell asleep at Terrance's house, and woke up in his bed, after sitting around having drinks with him.

Terrance was there for her when she needed a shoulder to lie on. When she was feeling insecure about Amanda, he was always her listening ear. Most importantly, when Neil went on long-distance trips, they would spend time together at his place. But she had never stayed the night with him, and their relationship was completely platonic.

She knew if Neil had Amanda up in his hotel bed caressing her and shared a kiss like the one that she and Terrance shared tonight, she would be clowning worst than Neil was.

Lela wrapped her arms around him, hugging him, inhaling the very essence of him, knowing this might be her last time feeling him this way. To her surprise, he let her get close enough to feel his warmth.

"I love you. I'm sorry for what I did," she said.

"What you did?" He let out an evil laugh. "So far, none of this is making sense. What exactly *did* you do? Why don't you just come out and say, 'I've been out screwing any man I can get my hands on while you are out putting in work and jerking off looking at my picture'?"

He got angrier as reality set in. "Say you've been putting it out there when I thought you were *my* hidden treasure. You've been cheating on me, just say it!"

He took her hands off of him and headed back to the bedroom. Throwing the suitcase he brought home earlier on the bed, he opened it and started unpacking his clothes.

When Lela noticed he was replacing his dirty clothes from the suitcase with clean clothes from their closet, she grabbed his arm, turning him to face her. "Baby, please don't...please don't leave." Her face was red and her eyes puffy.

He chuckled in disbelief. "I'm not leaving. *You* are."

"You're putting me out?" she asked, sounding as if she couldn't understand why he would do such a thing.

"From the looks of things, you already have somewhere to lay your head, so I'm just making this easy for you."

He looked straight through her and went to the kitchen to get some trash bags. He then walked over to her dresser and in one big swoosh emptied all of her things off the vanity into the trash bag. Louis Vuitton luggage, not today. He was making her leave with trash bags. He looked at her so cold a shiver went down her spine.

"Get a bag and get the rest of your stuff, because sons or no sons, I don't want to see you for a long time."

"Okay, you want to hear the truth?" she cried with nothing else to lose. "I cheated on you, but it was emotional, not physical. I never had sex with him. I just had someone to talk to when you were gone or working long hours. I would never let another man touch my body, and until tonight when he kissed me before I left his apartment, we have *never* been intimate. I always drew the line there. We were friends and that was it.

"You were always with Amanda, and I needed someone to be there for me. NaQuetta is always busy with her men, and Tonya is usually too busy to talk when I call. I felt lonely and he was convenient."

By the look on Neil's face, Lela saw that her revelation did not change the dynamics of the situation, so she reluctantly began packing her trash bag.

"I never meant to hurt you. You have to believe me. Can you please find it in your heart to give me another chance?" She turned him around to look at her and saw that his eyes were bloodshot.

"How could I be so stupid?" Neil posed the question to no one in particular. "All the times you were accusing me of sleeping with Amanda, you had a convenient man to talk to and *be there for you*. This is too much for one night. I need some time to think."

Neil's emotions were going haywire. On the one hand, he wanted to forgive his wife and hold her in his arms for the rest of the night. On the other hand, he felt betrayed to the tenth power.

"I'm leaving for tonight, but don't come back after you drop the kids off at school tomorrow. I want the kids to stay at home so they can have some semblance of a normal life. I will arrange to be here when they get out of school. Leave your key on the table when you leave in the morning." He grabbed his keys and coat and stormed out of the bedroom without another word.

Lela lay on the bedroom floor sobbing like a baby as she watched a disheveled Neil storm out of their bedroom. The front door closed loudly behind him. When she heard his car's engine moving further and further from their house, reality had her in a vice grip and all she could do was cry and pray for forgiveness.

★ ★ ★

Too embarrassed and exhausted to drive to his parents' home in Opelika and have to explain why he was showing up on their doorstep at six o'clock in the morning, and not wanting to involve any of his friends in his personal business, Neil checked himself into the Hilton Garden Inn.

His mother would have been riding his tail to find out every detail of what was causing her son's grief, and right now, he just wanted to be alone. A few hours ago, all he wanted to do was wrap his arms around his wife.

Everyone thought he had it all. The perfect job, wife, kids, house, and car...the American dream. "Little do they know."

He fell onto the hotel bed in total disbelief. He could not believe *his Lela* had been out creeping while he was working. Then he thought about just how much work he had been doing lately and how he was always away on business, always working late, always bringing work home.

His thoughts raced on about how Lela could have been spending many of her days and nights away with her faceless, nameless lover, and he missed her already.

On days when he was flourishing in the boardroom, someone else was breaking his wife off in the bedroom. He felt deceived in the worst way. He never thought he would find someone that he would fall in love, marry, and have children with in the first place. Now, three years and a lot of good memories later, he stood with a knife piercing his heart and hanging out of his back.

Just when he thought he had no one to turn to, he called the one person he knew he could depend on.

"Amanda? Hi, it's Neil."

"Hey, Neil. Is everything okay?

"Not really. I need someone to talk to. Do you mind if I come over?"

"Of course not. I'll be waiting on you."

33
Kicked Out

A fter listening to 'I told you so' from NaQuetta, Lela spent the next two weeks at NaQuetta's house in seclusion. She agreed with Neil that it would be best to let Antwan and Jalan stay home with him to cause as little anguish for the kids as possible. He saw no need in the children having to be shuffled around until he and Lela sorted out their issues. This arrangement was tearing Lela up on the inside. She lay curled up in NaQuetta's guestroom clinching a pillow most days, trying to come to grips with how her perfect life had changed so drastically.

Every time the phone rang, Lela prayed it would be Neil. When he dropped the kids off last weekend, he didn't even get out of the car to speak to Lela. And when she went home to try to talk to him, he would rush her out.

The phone rang, and the caller ID showed it was Tonya. Lela answered it and talked to her friend for the first time in over two weeks.

"Hello," Lela answered, trying to sound enthused for Tonya's benefit.

Tonya wasted no time giving her a piece of her mind. "Lela? I can't believe you would just up and stop calling me or taking my calls. I have even come down there to see you several times, and you wouldn't come out of that room. You need to snap out of it, especially if you plan to get your man back."

"So, I see Ma or Quetta has told you everything," Lela responded simply.

"Yes, your mother told me, and what were you thinking going out with Terrance?"

"I don't know. I wish I knew."

"Have you talked to Neil? Talk to him, Lela."

"Girl, you just don't know. I have tried to talk to him. He will not give me the time of day. I miss him so much. When he came by to bring the boys over here last weekend, he didn't even get out of the car. He only speaks to me if it has something to do with Jalan or Antwan. He has cut me out of his life completely. If he loved me so much, how could he let me go just like that? It was so easy for him to let go. I don't understand."

"I know you're hurt. You know I know how that feels. But you have to think about what he is going through." Tonya had dealt with her share of cheaters.

Lela's defeated voice softened a decibel. "I have thought about what he is going through. That is what's tearing me up the most."

"Lela, you are going to have to give him some time. What you did cut him deep. He probably doesn't know which way is up right about now. Quite frankly, I'm a bit surprised myself. I thought you two were happy in love."

"We were...I mean...I got caught up with Terrance. Old feelings came rushing back. I never should have spent my anniversary with him. That is where I should have drawn the line."

"Hold up. Rewind. You spent your anniversary with him?" Tonya did not believe her ears.

"Yeah, but it was totally innocent. Besides, Neil stood me up and rushed off for a private meeting with Miss Amanda. Terrance just happened to be available."

"We don't know if Neil has been double dipping with Amanda though, but we do know you were laid up with Terrance when your husband came waltzing into town looking for you."

"Don't remind me." Lela felt a wave of tears coming, so she grabbed her tissue box.

"I really messed up this time, didn't I?" A small piece of Lela's psyche wanted her friend to tell that what she did was not as bad as it seemed. She needed assurance that after finding a man as good as Neil, she did not throw it away for a few meals and a smile from Terrance, an old flame who did not appreciate her enough to keep the fire burning when he had her. No such assurance came from her friend, yet Tonya's words were comforting.

"Yes, but you'll get through it. First, pray for forgiveness, my friend. Everyday pray about it. Several times a day pray. This is just a test. The Lord knows what a beautiful relationship you have with Neil, and he knows all of our flaws. Just keep trying to talk to Neil and let God handle the rest."

"Since when did you get all philosophical?"

"If you must know, God has finally answered my prayers and I have found a special man that has been really good to me Lela. But girl, it didn't happen a minute before God showed me that everything I needed was Him. Once I stopped looking for a man, one showed up on my doorstep. Praise God!"

"At least one of us is happy. I'm glad for you. Who is he?"

"A close friend."

"Well, who is it?"

"You know I've always been in love with your cousin, but now we are official. He proposed to me a week ago."

"What! Trey? Oh, my God! Why didn't you tell me you and Trey were together, much less engaged?"

"Because you have not been accepting calls for two weeks, remember?"

"With things this serious, I know you've been together for more than two weeks?"

"Well, yeah. Okay you got me there."

"You two really pulled this one off. No one knew you two were even dating."

Tonya laughed. "Yeah, we did, didn't we?" Then, on a serious note, she added, "That's why I know you and Neil are going to make it through this. Trey tells me that since you and Neil broke up, his work ethic has gone down the drain, and all he does is talk about you. He is hurt, but he misses you."

Lela was in tears hearing the anguish her actions had caused her husband.

"I'll talk to you later, Tonya. Thanks for calling and checking up on me."

"Lela, keep your head up. Only bow it in prayer, girl, and like I said, you will make it through this. Your marriage will make it through this. Oh, and make sure your rendezvous with Mr. Terrance are over."

"That goes without saying. I want and need my husband back."

"I'll call you later today. My sweetie is at the door."

Lela hung up the phone. She had to talk to Neil. She pulled herself out of bed and looked at her disheveled appearance in the mirror. *"Dang, girl, it only takes you two weeks to turn into a complete bum."* Lela turned her nose up at her image in the mirror.

Lela stepped into the steamy shower and lathered soap all over her body. She used her lavender body wash and sponge ball to clean her body and then lathered up her hair with tea-tree shampoo. The warm water bouncing off her skin seemed to cleanse her of her wrongdoings.

In the guestroom, she dressed in blue jeans, a pink V-neck t-shirt, and tennis shoes. She blow dried her hair and curled it up in a flip. She put on a pair of platinum dangle earrings, and applied a layer of makeup, lip gloss, and eye shadow. Satisfied with her appearance, she prayed that Neil would listen to her when she made it home. Since it was Saturday and just before noon, she hoped he would be there and at least agree to talk.

Pulling into Pointe Shores, she could feel her spirits lift. *This was home.* She parked in the driveway and slowly walked up the sidewalk to the door. Before she could knock, Antwan opened the door.

"Momma!" He hugged her tight and started rambling about everything going on with him in school and sports. "I'm in the spelling bee. I won the first round at school yesterday."

"Oh, really!" Lela took Antwan in her arms and hugged him tightly. "I'm so proud of you. Mommy's going to have to be there for the next one. Where is Jalan?"

"Antwan, who are you talking to?" Neil asked, walking into the room. He placed a racquetball down on the coffee table and sat down on the loveseat. "Oh…hi, Lela."

"Neil, I need to talk to you."

"Now is not a good time," Neil said, preoccupied with gazing down the hall.

Lela took a seat beside Neil. "When is going to be a good time for you? You have been brushing me off for two weeks."

"I know now is not a good time, though."

"Mommy!" Jalan bounced into the room, riding on Amanda's hip. He jumped down to the floor and toddled over into his mother's arms. "Mommy. Me pway wa-ter."

Amanda's hair was wet, and she wore a bikini top and shorts. Lela figured they had just come back from Pointe Shores' indoor pool.

"That's nice, baby. Do you and Antwan want to go visit Auntie NaQuetta with Mommy?"

"Yes!" Antwan shouted.

"Uuh huh," Jalan followed suit.

"I wanna stay with you, Momma." Antwan's big, innocent eyes pierced through her heart.

"Neil, I'm going to take the boys to spend the night with me at NaQuetta's."

"I need to talk to you, Lela." Neil motioned for Lela to follow him into the den. Lela followed behind him with quick heavy steps.

"Antwan, go to your room and pick out an outfit for school tomorrow and put it in your backpack. Pack your brother an outfit, too. Don't forget socks and underwear," Lela instructed her son. She would be damned if she left them sitting with Amanda while she and Neil left the room. Amanda was already taking her place from the looks of things.

In the den, Lela could not believe her eyes. Amanda's pants and shirt were sprawled out all over the couch. Her panties and bra were hanging out of a gym bag. The more she stood there, she felt like this home was not hers but one that was sold, with new owners.

Lela spoke through clenched teeth. "So now you want to talk?! Well, what could you possibly want to talk about, Neil?" She didn't give him a chance to answer the question and continued blasting at him, "I'm taking my kids with me. This plan of keeping them in a *stable* home environment is not working out. Especially if you are going to have them playing house with Amanda. What, are you two phasing me out, already?"

"Don't come in here making demands and accusations. You gave up your right to make decisions in this house when you chose to leave it and go be with your other man. How is that working out for you? You expect the boys to shack up with you at NaQuetta's, or are you all going to move into Terrance Moore's studio apartment?"

Noting the shock on Lela's face, Neil added, "Yeah, I had your boy checked out. He wasn't hard to find either since he has called the house several times a day, hanging up each time. I guess he forgot about caller ID."

"Terrance has nothing to do with this. I have never taken my kids around him. He was nothing more than a friend. True, I went about our friendship all wrong, but that's all it was. But oh, how quickly Amanda has taken my place on your *pedestal*." Lela pointed to the gym bag that Amanda's pink thong underwear was hanging out of. "Now, this...this is different. It didn't take long for you two to show your true colors."

"Remember, this is what you started, Lela. Not that I owe you any explanation, but I have been lonely and sitting around the house because of *your* actions. Amanda picked up on it at work and came by the last few evenings to cheer me up. We've been playing board games and discussing you, mostly. Kind of like what Terrance did for you."

"I'm sorry, Neil, for all that I have done. I truly am sorry, but nothing cuts deeper than seeing the very woman who has tried to destroy us since day one be the person you turn to when the chips are down."

Feeling an internal storm brewing, Lela cut the conversation short saying, "I will just take my sons and go. I will take good care of them, like I always have, so you don't have to worry."

"Lela wait..." Neil stood there with his mouth open with the appearance that he had a lot to say, but could not produce the words.

Deflated, Lela walked down the familiar hall lined with family portraits and fought with every nerve ending in her body not to break down. The jasmine-scented air fresheners Lela put in the vents reminded her of when Neil would turn on the air conditioner just to smell the scent. Tiny spots in the carpet that were barely noticeable brought back the time when Antwan and Jalan served her breakfast in bed and Jalan had dripped OJ on the floor all the way to the bedroom. The house held so many cherished memories. Memories that Amanda's presence threatened to erase.

Lela packed enough clothes for the boys to last a week. While she packed, she overheard Neil talking to Amanda.

"The boys are going with Lela and I'm too exhausted to go to Anthony's like we planned, so I'll call you later if I change my mind."

"Are you sure you don't need me to stay and tidy up the place for you?"

"I'm sure. The maid service comes tomorrow, so don't worry about that. I'm sorry for the change in plans."

"We'll do something another time. Maybe tomorrow night I'll stop by?" Amanda purred, every word cutting Lela to the soul. Any other time, she would have had choice words for Amanda, but at this moment she didn't have anything left to fight with.

"I'll get back with you on that," Neil said halfheartedly.

Amanda passed by Jalan's bedroom door, heading to the den to retrieve her things, and Lela could read the smirk on her face. Amanda waved her hands and mouthed "Bye, bye" to Lela.

Lela opened the back door to her Jeep and bent over to position Jalan into his seat. She was having trouble adjusting the belt so that it fit around him snuggly.

"Let me help you with that." Neil stood closely behind Lela.

Lela turned around and stepped out of the way. Any other time, his closeness would have been welcomed, but her feelings were going haywire and desire was not one of them.

"Thanks," she said as she walked around and got in on the driver's seat. "Antwan, buckle up."

After adjusting Jalan in his seat, Neil walked around to the driver's window and tapped on it. Lela powered the window down. "Yes?"

"I don't want a divorce. I want you to come back home. I'm just not ready yet."

"Oh yeah? Well, don't call me when you're ready," Lela said, not meaning a word of it. If it were not for Amanda being there, she would have happily jumped at the thought.

34
Defining Moments

Terrance blew up Lela's cell phone the first week or so after Neil caught them, but Lela would not take his calls. When she finally did return his calls, she let him know that she was not interested in any type of relationship or contact with him.

To occupy her time, Lela started volunteering at Antwan's school the day after she brought them to stay with her at NaQuetta's.

A week later, she was sitting behind the secretary's chair in the office when the school's principal rushed into the office.

"Mrs. Johnston! We have a student that fell off the monkey bars and it doesn't look good. Call the ambulance now!"

Lela quickly dialed 9-1-1, and the operator dispatched an ambulance to the school. When she got off the phone, she asked, "What's the child's name so I can call his parents?"

"It's Antwan Johnston." In the principal's haste, he did not put two and two together that Antwan was Lela's son.

"Antwan Johnston! That's my son!" Lela nearly knocked the principal down as she ran to the monkey bars to Antwan.

Within five minutes, the ambulance was there and took over the care of Antwan. Lela sped to the hospital behind the ambulance, breaking every traffic law in the books. With Antwan being unconscious and still not having come around, his injury was considered serious.

"Lord, please be with my son. Please be with him. I can't go through this again."

At the hospital, they rushed him into the emergency room where the emergency physicians took over his care. Lela sat in the waiting room for twenty minutes before a nurse emerged from the back and gave her an update on his condition.

"Mrs. Johnston, there is good and bad news. The bad news is your son has a concussion and there is swelling around his brain from the impact of the fall. He has a hairline fracture of the skull, as well. The good news is that with a lot of rest and conventional healthcare he should pull through just fine. He is awake now and able to answer yes or no questions. He has feeling in his arms and legs, and those are good signs right now given the situation."

"Thank God!" Lela said as she released tears of joy.

Soon after the doctor walked away, Neil walked in and rushed over to Lela. "How is Antwan? Is he going to be all right?"

Lela recounted to Neil the news the nurse had given her. They stood entangled in each other's arms as they both prayed for their son. Ten minutes later, Amanda walked in with a 'Get Well' balloon.

"What the hell is she doing here?" Lela asked.

"Neil, why are you hugging her like that?" Amanda asked.

Lela looked back and forth between Neil and Amanda. Was Amanda questioning her husband about hugging her, and if so, why?

"First of all," he said to Lela, "Amanda insisted on driving me here because when the school called I was too shaken up to drive. Second of all," he turned to Amanda, "this is my wife, and I don't have to explain anything I do with my wife to you."

Lela felt Neil handled the situation well enough until Amanda added, "She wasn't being your wife last night, so why does she have to be today?"

"Amanda, you are tripping," was Neil's only response to Amanda's question. He turned to Lela and asked, "When are we going to be able to go back and see Antwan?"

"Don't even worry about it. How dare you bring your bitch in my face bragging about how she had you last night! He's not your son anyway, so if you will please leave, and take your white trash with you."

"Not my son! You really do play dirty, but you picked the wrong one to play with. Antwan *is* my son. Remember, I adopted him, so I have just as much a right to be here as you do."

"How dare you tell him that is not his son!" Amanda jumped in Lela's face, pointing her finger. "*You* are the piece of trash. Thank God for Terrance, because you really messed up a good thing, Lela, and a woman like me has been waiting in the wings for a long time. You can believe Neil is going to be well taken care of, so long as I have breath in my body."

"My son is fighting for his life, and you want to go on a rant about Terrance and what you are going to do for my husband!" Lela slapped Amanda with all the power within her body, and then turned to Neil. "Take your trifling bitch and go!"

Just then, security came rushing through a set of glass doors by the nurses' station to diffuse the situation, but by that time, Neil had escorted a swinging and kicking Amanda back to her car.

Through the window, Lela witnessed Amanda wrap her slender arms around Neil's neck and go in for a kiss. After a brief exchange, he pushed away.

Lela could not believe her eyes. The one woman she spent the last three and a half years trying to fight like a flea from her husband's ass had gotten just what she wanted, and it was all her fault. The most painful thing was there was nothing she could do about it, and at the moment she didn't want to do anything about it. Her energy was drained, but her baby needed her to be strong for him, and she would be.

She walked to Antwan's hospital room and felt as if a weight had been lifted. As long as her handsome boys were safe and secure, going back to single status may not be so bad.

35
Leave it to Grandma

Miss Rachel filled her mother in on Antwan's status. She let her know that he had been discharged from the hospital and was on bed rest for one week. She also let her mother in on what had been going on in her daughter's marriage.

"Lela and Neil done split up. He caught her out with another man," Rachel whispered.

"Hush your mouth! Lela wouldn't do anything like that," Grandma Jana said, quick to Lela's defense.

"Oh yes, she has, Momma. I heard it from the donkey's mouth."

"Well, she must have been going through some things that we don't know about, because I know my Lela, and she wouldn't do anything like that without a reason." Grandma Jana shook her head. "And she better have a good one to tell me when I get there."

"Get here? You coming down here, Momma."

"I most definitely am. I can't let my sweet pea go through all of this stress alone. She needs her grandma."

Grandma Jana called and made arrangements for lodging, and when her flight arrived, Neil stood in the airport waiting for her. Grandma Jana pulled him into a tight hug. "How is my favorite grandson-in-law?"

"Fine, but I'm your only grandson-in-law, aren't I?"

"All the same, all the same."

"So where are you headed? You want to go put up your things

first, or do you want me to take you to see Lela?"

"To put up my things."

After two weeks of hard work, the McGhee deal folded. Neil did not even see it coming, and he was floored. Don't get it wrong; he'd lost an account before, but he had never been intentionally sabotaged.

Amanda, on the other hand, was not surprised. She was on cloud nine with her twisted revenge, seeing as how she purposely altered the presentation figures, causing Neil to lose the account.

Neil had the board of directors of McGhee Enterprises eating out of his hand. This deal would have opened new doors for Naytek that could have taken the company to the next level. Not only would they have been selling transcription services, but also billing services.

After explaining to the McGhee decision makers that he would get the correct figures to them by the next morning, he flipped on the projector to do his presentation and pictures of Lela and Terrance laughing over lunch at Chili's Restaurant popped upon the screen. The pictures that Amanda snapped from across the room the first day Terrance and Lela ran into each other at the beauty salon were well defined and unmistakably a lunch date.

People in the room who knew Neil's wife sat silently. Others wondered what the pictures had to do with the presentation. Neil pressed the blue button vigorously, eager to see picture after picture. The very last one showed Terrance kissing his wife in the parking lot of Chili's.

"What the..." Neil was to baffled to finish the meeting. He sat down in his chair and announced that the meeting would have to be rescheduled.

"Will all due respect, this has been an utter waste of time Mr. Johnston. If we can't get down to business today, then don't worry about calling us back in the future," the McGhee representative was blunt.

Amanda's nonchalance showed more than she would ever tell. She just sat there in her chair twirling her pen as if she were a part of the furnishings.

Indifferent to the consequences, Neil gathered his laptop, which had the disk with the images of his wife and her lover, and walked out of the boardroom.

Back in her office, Amanda paced the floor. "That'll teach him to move Lela's grandmother in with him and then ignore me. I'm glad he lost the deal, and the look on his face when he saw the pictures, priceless," she laughed. "Cornelius Johnston needed to be reminded that I'm the best thing for him."

* * *

Grandma Jana had Amanda's number, and after a little investigative work of her own, she was ready to take her down.

"Neil, I've got something I need to show you," Grandma Jana said to Neil after eating a pancake breakfast the morning after he lost the McGhee account.

"What you got, Grandma?"

"Well, you know that girl from your office? I've had my eye on her ever since I noticed her acting sour at your wedding. I had a feeling from the beginning that she would be at the root of some of you and sweet pea's problems."

"What are you saying?"

"Look at these and see what you can figure out." Grandma slid Neil a manila folder and watched as he looked over the pictures.

"What is this supposed to mean? So what if Amanda has a black boyfriend." The pictures showed Amanda straddling a dark-skinned brother in an upscale hotel room.

"Not just any boyfriend, but that's Terrance Moore."

"The same Terrance that is Lela's friend? I guess I can see the resemblance from the pictures that mysteriously ended up in my boardroom presentation."

"They are one in the same. And that's not the most shocking evidence. Look at what I have highlighted from Amanda's bank records."

"That's weird. Why would Amanda pay him five thousand dollars last month?"

"Amanda's a smart girl, but old Grandma Jana is wise. Choose wisdom over wits any day, son. I hired a private investigator, and he found out that Amanda paid Terrance to come in and shake up you and Lela's marriage in order for her to do damage control. The girl sleeps with a picture of you on her pillow. She lives and breathes Cornelius Johnston, and she has been ready to get rid of Lela for a long time. In searching her house, he found this." Grandma Jana handed Neil two diaries. "Read it when you get a chance, and you will get the answer to some of the problems you and Lela have had over the last few years."

Neil took the diary and went to his bedroom, where he lay across the bed reading entry after entry.

December 23, 2004
Just when I thought things could not get any worse, I come home to a
Dear Jane letter from Kent. I am hurting so bad right now. I could
just end it all. Amanda

December 30, 2004
Kent has been ignoring my messages I left at his job. He even
changed his cell phone number. I know it is that secretary of his that
he left me for. Don't worry, she will get hers and so will he. I had to
get out, so I went for drinks tonight. A guy who says he works for
Naytek was there. The poor thing looked almost as sad as I am. He's
a black guy, but kind of cute. At least I have my new job to look
forward to. Amanda

Neil read through entries about dieting, work, and other personal
things, until he came across an entry with his name.

June 4, 2005
I've been working with Neil for almost six months now and my
attraction is growing stronger and stronger for him. I don't know
what it is, but this guy has my nose wide open. I use work as an
excuse to spend any time that I can with him. I called him all day
today to see if we could meet. Looks like I'll be going over to his
place tomorrow because he's at Trey's family reunion. So that leaves
me with nothing but his picture to put me to sleep. One day, I'll have
love in my life again. Amanda

Neil skimmed through the pages until he found the source of
the dagger hanging out of his back.

December 10, 2005
I can't believe he showed me the ring that he bought for Lela. Can he
not see that my heart bleeds for him? He is actually considering
marrying that…that woman. I've let this little fling go on long
enough. It is time for me to do something about it. After tonight, Neil
won't know what hit him, but he will definitely not be looking back.
Mend your heart,
Amanda

December 11, 2005
My plan worked! The sleeping pill knocked Neil out, and allowed me
to have my way with him. I did everything imaginable, but I didn't
have intercourse with him, though. When I give myself completely to
him, I want him to be fully aware of it. I want him to know and feel
everything I have to offer. Oh, I know he wants me, he just hasn't
realized it yet. And Lela, how pathetic. She fell right in step with my
plan. She is so damn predictable, anyway. When I called and told her
that Neil needed her to come down, she didn't even question me. She
should know by now that I don't have any good intentions for her. I
will not be denied. The only reason he would allow me in his house
that late at night with champagne is because he wants me. I know he
does. The look on Lela's face when she caught us this morning...now
that was priceless. LOL. I made sure she could tell by looking at me
that I just rolled out of his bed...and even Neil thinks he put it on
me. I'm sure he'll want seconds. Amanda

Neil clenched his fist. Amanda had doped him up the night she
was in his house. "I knew there was no way I would have had her in
my bed!"

It took Neil two days to read the entire diary, but finally, the one
thing that Grandma Jana wanted him to see was revealed. Amanda
intentionally kept Neil in the office to keep him away from his wife.
She also paid Terrance Moore to spend time with his lonely wife
who was lonely because Amanda kept him in the office. Amanda
meticulously manipulated each business trip with her uncle so that
she and Neil would be together and planned tirelessly to seduce him.
He was livid.

Armed with the truth, Neil entered Naytek the following Monday
in blue jeans and a t-shirt. In his arms were the two diaries. He
barged into Amanda's office, nearly tearing the door off the hinges.

Amanda sat behind her desk with papers piled on top of each
other. She wore a black business suit and her hair was pulled into a
bun.

"Neil, what's the problem? Is it Antwan?"

"No, it's you! How dare you console me after fucking up my
marriage?" He threw the diaries on her desk.

"How did you get those? These are my personal things. Have
you been in my house?" Amanda's face emitted fright.

"How I got them is not as important as what I read in them."
Neil paced back and forth in front of her desk. "Why would you try

to ruin my marriage, especially when I've told you how much Lela means to me? I thought you were my friend. Why would you deliberately push my wife into the arms of another man?"

"I didn't push her anywhere. She was putty in Terrance's hands the first day he took her to lunch. You should have seen them together, like old lovers."

"That's not true and you know it. I have read in here, account after account, of how you deliberately planned things so that my wife could be alone and Terrance would be conveniently there for her. Not to mention the time you doped me up to sleep with me. You are a lunatic! And I am going to make sure Christian knows about it."

"Make sure I know about what?" Amanda's uncle appeared beside Neil. "What is the matter?"

Amanda got up from her desk and rushed to Neil's opposite side. "Neil, this is not necessary. We can talk about this later."

Ignoring Amanda, Neil spoke to his boss. "Christian, I will have my two-week notice on your desk by five o'clock. I cannot work with Amanda another day. She has been working overtime to sabotage my marriage, and the diaries on her desk prove it."

Amanda picked the diaries up off the desk and clinched onto them tightly. "That is ludicrous." Amanda put on an innocent face and giggled at Neil's accusation. "Why would I do a silly thing like that? Neil, we have worked together for years, and you *know* I respect you and your family."

"Neil, explain what you are saying?" Christian was utterly confused.

"I'm saying if you take a look at the diaries in Amanda's hand, you will find the reason why I am leaving." Then to Amanda, Neil said, "I won't play your little game any longer."

"Christian, if it is not a problem I will be working from home the next two weeks tying up any loose ends. If you have any specific requests of me, let me know." Neil then left the office, but not before shooting Amanda one last disgusted look.

Neil left Naytek and headed straight to NaQuetta's house. When Lela opened the door, he hugged her tightly.

Lela didn't know whether to be happy to see her husband, or if something tragic had happened to cause him to come to her with open arms.

"I'm sorry, Lela. I'm so sorry for the way I have treated you. I want you and the boys to come home."

Neil and Lela had a long talk about where things went wrong in their marriage. They discussed everything concerning Terrance and Amanda, the outside forces that were causing the rift between them.

Leaving Naytek was a hard pill for Neil to swallow, but the decision was not hard when he laid all of his cards on the table. When it came down to it, his family was more important than his career.

Antwan had completely healed from his concussion and was back in school. He and Jalan were happy to be home, but not as happy as Lela. Having her family together meant more than any consolation another man could give her.

Sitting around the dinner table, Lela, Neil, Antwan, Jalan, and Grandma Jana enjoyed a huge meal. After dinner, while sitting in the den, Jalan asked, "Ganma, you stay with us?"

"No baby, Grandma Jana is going back home to Cali in the morning," Grandma Jana replied.

"We would love for you to stay, and you know you are welcome here. Well, in our new home in Opelika." Neil said.

"Come on, Grandma. We'll have plenty of room, and you would be close to family," Lela begged.

"When I'm too old to do anything for myself, I'll move into your extra room, baby, but until then, Grandma Jana has her own life to lead. Besides, you will have your hands full with your husband, and I can sense a new baby on the horizon. A girl."

Lela and Neil looked at each other with wide eyes before Neil spoke up. "Wait a minute now. I just walked out on my job. We can't handle another child right now." Neil figured they could live comfortably off of his savings and severance package for a couple years, but then something would have to give.

"Young folks, I tell you. You can handle anything God puts on you. Now, I'm going to tell you two like I told Lela in the beginning, because Grandma Jana is not always going to be around to keep this thing tight for you. Never let anyone come in between you two. Marriage is sacred and you should always honor each other before anyone else.

"Neil, I know you felt like work was the most important thing in life. That's why Amanda could call you any time of the day and take you away from your family, but there is only room for one leading lady in a man's life.

"Lela, you, my dear, felt neglected and found attention you were not getting at home in another man. That's where you went wrong. No matter how the chips are falling, you don't turn to another man.

Turn to God."

In the middle of their conversation, Neil answered his buzzing cell phone.

Lela heard him say, "Hello. Yes, sir. No, sir. Really! I have to talk to my wife first, but that sounds good. I appreciate you, too. I will give you a call back tomorrow with the specifics.

"That was Christian Broady. He doesn't want to see me leave the company, so not only did he offer me a transfer back to Opelika, but he's appointing me chief financial officer over that branch!"

Antwan jumped up and down at the thought of moving closer to his grandmother Rachel and his old friends.

"And that's not the best part. He has transferred Amanda to the New York branch and assured me that our work should not cause us to have to intermingle any more than I was comfortable with."

"Are you going to take it?" Lela asked containing her excitement.

"Well, I told him I would talk to you first. Do you want to move back to Opelika?"

"What, are you crazy? Of course, I do. I miss Tonya and momma so much. I would be so happy to be around *all* of the people I care about. The only reason I moved to Atlanta was to be with you, but if I can have you and be in Opelika, too, then I'm on top of the world." Lela turned to her grandmother and said, "Now, I just have to work on grandma."

Grandma Jana only smiled at Lela's suggestion. Her flight was due to leave in the morning, and she would definitely be on it.

Neil pulled Lela up off the sofa, gave her a peck on the lips, and whispered in her ear, "Then it's settled. I will call him in the morning." Then he pulled her by the hand and said, "come on. Let's go to bed."

"Grandma, you want me to put the boys to bed now?"

Grandma Jana smiled knowingly and said, "No. I will put them to bed in a little while. You two go on and go to *sleep*."

Lela and Neil exited the room headed to the master bedroom. Satisfied that she succeeded in her mission, Grandma Jana rubbed Antwan's head lovingly and thought, *"A grandmother's work is never done."*

A Duet

Poetry by Joi Marsh

We are minds interlocking
Reaching and gathering information
In constant search for salvation
We store all we can
Waiting for our day…to release it all
In an explosion of ecstasy
Shared elations
Intimate moments and transformations
Caressing 'til sunrise
And well into midday
On a bed of roses
With scents of love
Where two beats become one
Exchanging air
So close
So sweet …such desire
Setting afire
Traditions leaving inhibitions
And fears behind
As in unorthodox manners
We locate satisfaction…completion
I believe I have found that
In you
A Soul Mate

Following are Chapters 1 and 2 of my sophomore novel, Secrets of a Kept Woman. In Secrets Of a Kept Woman, Shayla Wilson is married to the biggest drug dealer in town. Their lifestyle is lavish, but the flames are all but dead in their marriage. He married Shayla because of her beauty and treats her like a trophy – up on a pedestal and rarely touched. All of that is fine and good, but Shayla is in dyer need of attention, love and affection. When Antonio drops in to do some pool maintenance work, he services a few tubes for Shayla and the rest is a wrap. The secrets of a kept woman can be deadly if revealed...

Secrets of a Kept Woman

Chapter 1

Mrs. Wilson

"Since the moment Titus gave me the title *Mrs.* Wilson, he has slowly pushed me to the back." Shayla had called her best friend to vent about her husband's latest no-call, no-show to a date that *he* planned together for them.

She paused taking a moment to assimilate the ambience she set for the evening. Her Jacuzzi, positioned in the middle of their jumbo gazebo in the backyard, was flowing with warm bubbly water scented with a touch of jasmine oil. The gazebo was outlined by dim post lighting that created a sensual ambience. Pink floating candles at the four corners of the gazebo along with an assortment of designer candles around the Jacuzzi made for an added effect. She succeeded in turning their backyard into a lover's paradise.

All of this and no one to share it with, she thought.

"I can't believe I let myself fall for his BS again. Titus never shows up when he makes plans with me," Shayla whined making her lips more pouty than usual.

Rhonda listened to her friend attentively only speaking when asked a direct question. She knew what Shayla needed right now was someone to listen to her talk.

"If I didn't have his platinum and diamond ring on my right ring finger, I would have to know I was just some side-show action. I hope he doesn't think that I'm going to continue to sit around waiting for him Ronnie. He needs to recognize what's here at home. Or maybe I should be asking myself is this really *his* home." Shayla complained in a tangent to her lifelong best friend.

Rhonda remained silent.

"I guess I did all of this for nothing then," she continued to hold a conversation by herself, not picking up on the fact that her friend was oddly silent.

Shayla slid open the patio door and entered her two-story Victorian lakeside home. She talked for another 20 minutes with Rhonda. Then finally Rhonda offered up some consolation.

"Girl, you know Titus is hustling. He is a don in these streets and he has to be in the streets to make things happen, so don't stress it when he has to be out there. Like tonight, he's probably handling some business. Don't you like living on Society Hill Shores?"

"I do, but that doesn't change the fact that I need him with me sometimes. I'm not asking for much to get one night out of the week with him. I mean I put up with a lot. I didn't get married to be lonely. I would give all of this up in a heartbeat if I could have him here with me." Shayla said at the brink of tears.

"Listen, I'm sure he'll be home soon. He always makes it back home to *you* girl. Try calling him again. Maybe he was just tied up." Rhonda chastised in her usual demeanor.

Easing up on her now sobbing friend, Rhonda added, "even better, he's probably picking you up a gift. You know how he likes to buy you things." Just as that last statement rolled off her tongue, Rhonda rolled her eyes hoping her jealousy did not emanate in her voice.

"You have to think on the bright side girl," Rhonda continued. She was dead set on convincing Shayla of Titus' faithfulness. "It *is* your finger he put the ring on."

Shayla twirled her hair with while pacing the floor.

"You're right, he does spoil me and he did make me Mrs. Wilson." She smiled. "I guess I wouldn't be complaining if I was getting sexed more often." Shayla laughed through tears.

"I am married to one of the, no *the*, biggest hustler in town, he's fine and he knows what to do when he does what he do, if you know what I'm talkin' bout. Yet I can't get anything to jump off in the bedroom, and trust I have tried everything."

Shayla laughed thinking of her assortment of Victoria Secret lingerie, creams, flavored panties and powders and the swing she had installed in the shower a few weeks ago. For the first time during the conversation, her mood picked up. She took a look around at all of their high-end possessions.

"All of this stuff is nice, but let's face it, I can't make love to a flat screen TV, chinchilla, or Chanel pumps. I need some time and attention from my man. Hell, I would get some on the low but I can't even do that. He's got every eye in town watching me like a hawk. I can't sneeze without him knowing it."

It had been at least two weeks since she and Titus had sex and before then three weeks. This latest stint was due to him being on a weeklong run to Cali on business. Then when he returned to town he spent the first few days catching up with street collections. A blind man could see that money was his first love.

Here it was tonight Shayla planned to show him exactly what he had been missing at home. But like so many other nights, he was a no-call, no-show, and to plans that *he* made. To top it off he didn't have the decency to call. Shayla was beginning to wonder why she put up with his antics.

When they first got together three years ago Titus had a high sex drive. On the real tip, he was a sex fiend, so she knew there was no way he was going two weeks, pushing three, without busting a grape.

She walked through the kitchen into the den and sat on her plush leather sectional sofa with the phone close to her ear.

"Calm down Lay. Don't be giving him a hard time when he gets home either. At least give him a chance to explain," Rhonda spurted in Titus' defense.

"He hasn't even called Ronnie. How could you be so supportive of him? I have called his cell ten times already and he didn't answer. This is really getting old and I'm not getting any younger." Shayla confided in her friend.

"Yes, but think about the end when he doesn't have to hustle like that anymore. You'll be able to appreciate what he is doing then." *If you don't I'm sure I can think of at least one other person who will,* Rhonda thought as she continued to give Shayla excuses Titus' behavior.

If Shayla didn't know any better, she would guessed Rhonda had a little attitude with her last comment. If she knew one thing for sure and two things for certain, it was that Rhonda always had a stack full of excuses for Titus. She would say, "*He's a baller. Girl do not lose your good thing. You should be glad for what he does for you. Don't be worrying that man about that. He's this, he's that.*" Ronnie was part of the reason she had put up with Titus' lifestyle as long as she had, but she was beginning to wonder if Rhonda was her friend *or his*.

Giving that they had been friends since grade school Shayla never felt the need to question Rhonda's reasoning. She knew her friend was just trying to help her keep her marriage intact.

"Well girl, I'm going to let you go. No need in both of us having a depressing Friday night. I'm sure you're about to get your club on or something."

Shayla missed her clubbing and hanging out days, but Titus kept her on a tight leash. He was the leader of the local drug ring and said it would have looked weak on his part for his lady to be in a club, unless she was by his side, so he forbade her from clubbing or going out with her friends unless it was pre-approved by him.

"No actually, I had a little company earlier, so I'm going to be getting some much needed rest tonight."

"Oh, it was that good, huh? Anyone that can keep Rhonda the Diva away from the Club Diamond on a Friday night must be *putting it down*." They both laughed.

You do know what you're saying, Rhonda thought. She began to speak but Shayla cut her off.

"Let me guess. You found some prime real estate up in Club Diamond last week?"

Ronda was once again silent.

"Well don't be all secretive give up the goods, who is he? Do I know him?" Shayla said excitedly.

"Let's not get into all that Miss Thang. I'll tell you all about him one day soon. Listen, I'll talk to you tomorrow," Rhonda said speedily. She was all of a sudden brief and ready to go.

"Coo..." Dial tone. Shayla hung up the phone. Her friend's succinctness was odd, but she brushed it off. She had her own problems to deal with, like Mr. Titus and his whereabouts.